KIDNAP THE

OTHER TITLES IN THE SAS OPERATION SERIES

Behind Iraqi Lines
Mission to Argentina
Sniper Fire in Belfast
Desert Raiders
Samarkand Hijack
Embassy Siege
Guerrillas in the Jungle
Secret War in Arabia
Colombian Cocaine War
Invisible Enemy in Kazakhstan
Heroes of the South Atlantic
Counter-insurgency in Aden
Gambian Bluff
Bosnian Inferno
Night Fighters in France
Death on Gibraltar
Into Vietnam
For King and Country
Kashmir Rescue
Guatemala – Journey into Evil
Headhunters of Borneo
War on the Streets
Bandit Country
Days of the Dead

SAS
OPERATION

Kidnap the Emperor!

JAY GARNET

HARPER

Harper
An imprint of HarperCollins*Publishers*
1 London Bridge Street,
London SE1 9GF
www.harpercollins.co.uk

This paperback edition 2016
1

First published by 22 Books/Bloomsbury Publishing plc 1994

Copyright © Bloomsbury Publishing plc 1994

Jay Garnet asserts the moral right to
be identified as the author of this work

A catalogue record for this book
is available from the British Library

ISBN: 978 0 00 815527 8

Products carrying the FSC label are independently certified
to assure consumers that they come from forests that are managed
to meet the social, economic and ecological needs
of present and future generations.

Find out more about HarperCollins and the environment at
www.harpercollins.co.uk/green

Prologue

Addis Ababa, Ethiopia.

'Haile Selassie, former Emperor of Ethiopia, who was deposed in a military coup last year, died in his sleep here yesterday aged 83. A statement by Ethiopian radio said he died of an illness after a prostate gland operation two months ago. He was found dead by attendants yesterday.'

The Times, 28 August 1975

April 1976
North and east of Addis Ababa lies one of the hottest places on earth. Known as the Afar or Danakil Depression, after two local tribes, it points like an arrowhead tempered by the desert sun southwards from the Red Sea towards the narrow gash of Africa's Rift Valley.

For hundreds of square miles the plain is unbroken but for scanty bushes whose images shimmer above the scorched ground. Occasionally here and there a gazelle browses, wandering between meagre thorn bushes across rock or sand streaked with sulphur from the once volcanic crust.

Even in this appalling wilderness, far from the temperate and beautiful highlands more often associated with Ethiopia,

1

there are inhabitants. Most are herders who wander the scattered water-holes. But some make a precarious living trading slabs of salt levered from the desert floor – some five million years ago the depression was a shallow inlet of the Red Sea and its retreat left salty deposits that still cake the desert with blinding white. Camels transport the blocks to highland towns.

Soon after dawn on the morning of 19 April, a caravan of ten camels, groaning under grey slabs of salt done up in protective matting, set off from their camp along unpaved tracks towards the highlands. There were three drovers – two teenagers and their father, a bearded forty-five-year-old whose features seemed parched into premature old age by the desert sun. His name was Berhanu, not that it was known to anyone much beyond his immediate family.

Yet before the week was out it would be known, briefly, to a number of the Marxists who had seized power from the Emperor Haile Selassie eighteen months previously, and most importantly to Lieutenant-Colonel Mengistu Haile Mariam, then number two in the government but in effect already the country's implacably ruthless leader. A record of Berhanu's name may still exist in a Secret Police file in 10 Duke of Harar Street, Addis Ababa, along with a brief description of what Berhanu experienced that day.

The caravan had just rounded a knoll of rock. It was approaching midday. Despite a gusty breeze, the heat was appalling – 120 degrees in the shade. Berhanu, as usual at this time, called a halt, spat dust from his lips, and pointed off the road to a small group of doum-palms that would provide shade. He knew the place well. So did the camels. Nearby there was a dip that would hold brackish water.

With the camels couched, the three sought relief from the heat in the shade of the trees. The two boys dozed. It was then that Berhanu noticed, in the trembling haze two or three hundred yards away, a group of circling vultures. He would not have looked twice except that the object of their attention was still moving.

And it was not an animal.

He stared, in an attempt to make sense of the shifting image, and realized he was looking at a piece of cloth being seized and shaken by the oven-hot gusts. Unwillingly he rose, and approached it. As he came nearer, he saw that the cloth was a cloak, and that the cloak seemed to be concealing a body. It had not been there all that long, for the vultures had not yet begun to feed. They retreated at his approach, awaiting a later chance.

The body was tiny, almost childlike, though the cloth – which he now saw was a cloak of good material – would hardly have been worn by a child.

Berhanu paused nervously. Few people came to this spot. It was up to him to identify the corpse, for he would no doubt have to inform some grieving family of their loss. He walked over to the bundle, squatted down and laid the flapping cloak flat along the body, which was lying on its face. He put a hand on the right shoulder, and rolled the body towards him on to its back.

The sight made Berhanu exhale as if he had been punched in the stomach. His eyes opened wide, in shock, like those of a frightened horse. For the face before him, sunken, emaciated, was that of his Emperor, Haile Selassie, the Power of Trinity, Conquering Lion of Judah, Elect of God, King of Kings of Ethiopia. Berhanu had known little of Ethiopia's steady collapse into poverty, of the reasons for the growing unrest against the Emperor, of the brutalities of the revolution. To him, Selassie was the country's father. As a child he

3

had honoured the Emperor's icon-like image on coins and medals inherited from his ancestors. And eight months previously he had ritually mourned the Emperor's death.

Berhanu felt panic rising in him. He fell to his knees, partly in adulation before the semi-divine countenance, and partly in a prayer for guidance. He began to keen softly, rocking backwards and forwards. Then abruptly he stopped. Questions formed. The presence of the corpse at this spot seemed miraculous. It must have been preserved, uncorrupted, for the best part of a year, and then somehow, for reasons he could not even guess at, transported here. Preserved where? Was he alone in seeing it? Was there some plot afoot upon which he had stumbled? Should he bury the body? Keep silent or report its presence?

Mere respect dictated that the body, even if divinely incorruptible, should be protected. Then, since others might already know of his presence here, he would show his innocence by making a report. Perhaps there would even be a reward.

Slowly, in the quivering heat, Berhanu gathered rocks and piled them in reverence over the body. Then he walked back, still trembling. He woke his sons, told them what he had seen and done, cursed them for unbelievers until they believed him, and hurried them on their way westwards.

Three days later, he delivered his consignment of salt, which would be sold in the local market for an Ethiopian dollar a slab. He collected his money, and went off with his sons to the local police chief.

The policeman was sceptical, and at first dismissed Berhanu as a madman. Then he became nervous – for peculiar things had been happening in this remote part of Tigré province over the past two years – and made a telephone call to his superiors in Addis.

From there, the bare bones of the report – that deep in the Danakil a local herder named Berhanu had found a corpse resembling the former Emperor – went from department to department. At each stage a bureaucrat decided the report was too wild to be taken seriously; and at each stage the same men decided in turn that they would not be the ones to say so. Within three hours the *éminence grise* of the revolution, Mengistu Haile Mariam, knew of it. He also knew, for reaons that will become apparent, that the report had to be true.

For the sake of the revolution, both the report and the evidence for its existence had to be eradicated. Mengistu at once issued a rebuke to every department involved, stating the report was clearly a fake, an error that should never have been taken seriously.

Secondly, he ordered the cairn to be visited and the contents destroyed. The following morning, a helicopter containing a senior army officer and two privates flew to the spot. The two privates unloaded a flame-thrower, and incinerated the cairn. The team had specific orders not to look beneath the stones, and never knew the purpose of their strange mission.

Thirdly, Mengistu ordered the disappearance of Berhanu and his sons. The police in Tigré had become used to such orders, and asked no questions. The three were found, fed, flattered, transported to a nearby army base with promises of money for their excellent work, and never heard of again. A cousin made enquiries a week later, but was met with bland expressions of sympathy.

The explanation for the presence of the Emperor's body in the desert in a remote corner of his country eight months after his death had been officially announced might therefore have remained hidden for ever.

There was, as Mengistu himself well knew, a possible risk. One other man knew the truth. But Mengistu had reason to think that he too was dead, a victim of the desert.

The existence of this book proves him wrong.

1

Thursday, 18 March 1976

The airport of Salisbury, Rhodesia, was a meagre affair: two terminals, hangars, a few acres of tarmac. Just about right for a country whose white population was about equal to that of Lewisham in size and sophistication, pondered Michael Rourke, as he waited disconsolately for his connection to Jo'burg.

Still, those who had inherited Cecil Rhodes's imperial mantle hadn't done so badly. Across the field stood a flight of four FGA9s, obsolete by years compared with the sophisticated beauties of the USA, Russia, Europe and the Middle East, but quite good enough at present to control the forested borderlands of Mozambique. And on the ground, Rhodesia had good fighting men, white and black, a tough army, more than a match for the guerrillas. But no match for the real enemy, the politicians who were busy cutting the ground from under the whites.

Rourke sank on to his pack, snapped open a tin of lager and sucked at it morosely. He had been in and out of the field for twelve years since first joining the SAS from the Green Jackets: Rhodesia on unofficial loan, for the last two

7

years; before that, Oman; before that, Aden. In between, back
to the Green Jackets.

The money here had not been great. But he'd kept fit and
active, and indulged his addiction to adrenalin without serious
mishap. At thirty-four his 160lb frame was as lean and hard
as it had been ten years earlier.

But now he had had enough of this place. He was tired:
tired of choppers, tired of the bush. The only bush he was
interested in right now belonged to Lucy Seymour, who hid
her assets beneath a virginal white coat in a chemist's down
the Mile End Road.

The last little jaunt had decided him.

There had been five of them set down in Mozambique by
a South African Alouette III Astazou. His group – an American,
another Briton and two white Rhodesians – were landed at
dusk in a clearing in Tete, tasked to check out a report that
terrorists – 'ters', as the Rhodesian authorities sneeringly called
them – were establishing a new camp near a village somewhere
in the area. Their plan was to make their way by night across
ten miles of bush, to be picked up the next morning. Four of
them, including the radio operator, were all lightly armed with
British Sterling L2A3 sub-machine-guns. One of the Rhodesians
carried an L7 light machine-gun in case of real trouble.

Rourke anticipated no action at all. The information was
too sparse. Any contact would be pure luck. All they would
do, he guessed, was establish that the country along their line
of march was clear.

But things hadn't gone quite as he thought they would. They
had moved a mile away from the landing zone and treated
themselves to a drink from their flasks, then moved on
cautiously. It was slow work, edging through the bush guided
between shadow and deeper shadow by starlight alone. Though

they could scarcely be heard from more than twenty yards away, their progress seemed to them riotous in the silent air – a cacophony of rustling fatigues, grating packs, the dull chink and rattle of weaponry. To penetrate their cocoon of noise, they stopped every five minutes and listened for sounds borne on the night air. Towards dawn, when they were perhaps a mile from their pick-up point, Rourke ordered a rest among some bushes.

They were eating, with an occasional whispered comment, when Rourke heard footsteps approaching. He peered through the foliage and in the soft light of the coming dawn saw a figure, apparently alone. The figure carried a rifle.

He signalled for two others, the American and the Briton, to position themselves either side of him, and as the black came to within thirty feet of their position he called out: 'All right. Far enough'. The figure froze.

Rourke didn't want to shoot. It would make too much noise.

'Do as we tell you and you won't be hurt. Put your gun on the ground and back away. Then you'll be free to go'.

That way, they would be clear long before the guerrilla could fetch help, even if there were others nearby.

Of course, there was no way of telling whether the black had understood or not. They never did know. Unaccountably, the shadowy shape loaded the gun, clicking the bolt into place. It was the suicidal action of a rank amateur.

Without waiting to see whether the weapon was going to be used, the three men, following their training and instinct, opened fire together. Three streams of bullets, perhaps 150 rounds in all, sliced across the figure, which tumbled backwards into the grass.

In the silence that followed, Rourke realized that the victim was not dead. There was a moan.

The noise of the shooting would have carried over a mile in the still air. He paused only for a moment.

'Wait one,' he said.

He walked towards the stricken guerrilla. It was a girl. She had been all but severed across the stomach. He caught a glimpse of her face. She was perhaps fifteen or sixteen, a mere messenger, probably with no experience of warfare, little training and no English. He shot her through the head.

He would have been happy to make it his war; he would have been happy to risk his life for a country that wasn't his; but he was not happy to lose. The place was going to the blacks anyway. So when they offered to extend his contract, when they showed him the telex from Hereford agreeing that he could stay on if he wished, he told them: thanks, but no thanks. There was no point being here any more.

Now he was going home, for a month's R and R, during which time he fully intended to rediscover a long-forgotten world, the one that lay beneath Lucy's white coat.

The clock on the Royal Exchange in the heart of the City of London struck twelve. Two hundred yards away, in a quiet courtyard off Lombard Street, equidistant from the Royal Exchange and the Stock Exchange, Sir Charles Cromer stood in his fifth-floor office, staring out of the window. Beyond the end of the courtyard, on the other side of Lombard Street, a new Crédit Lyonnais building, still pristine white, was nearing completion. To right and left of it, and away down other streets, stood financial offices of legendary eminence, bulwarks of international finance defining what was still a medieval maze of narrow streets.

Cromer, wearing a well-tailored three-piece grey suit and his customary Old Etonian tie, was a stocky figure, his bulk still heavily muscled. One of the bulldog breed, he liked to think. He stuck out his lower lip in thought and turned to walk slowly round his office.

As City offices went, it was an unusual place, reflecting the wealth and good taste of his father and grandfather. It also expressed a certain cold simplicity. The floor was of polished wood. To one side of the ornate Victorian marble fireplace were two sofas of button-backed Moroccan leather. They had been made for Cromer's grandfather a century ago. The sofas faced each other across a rectangular glass table. On the wall, above the table, beneath its own light, was a Modigliani, an early portrait dating from 1908. In the grate stood Cromer's pride and joy, a Greek jug, a black-figure amphora of the sixth century BC. The fireplace was now its showcase, intricately wired against attempted theft. The vase could be shown off with two spotlights set in the corners of the wall opposite. Cromer's desk, backing on to the window, was of a superb cherrywood, again inherited from his grandfather.

Cromer walked to the eight-foot double doors that led to the outer office and flicked the switch to spotlight the vase, in preparation for his next appointment. It was causing him some concern. The name of the man, Yufru, was unknown to him. But his nationality was enough to gain him immediate access. He was an Ethiopian, and the appointment had been made by him from the Embassy.

Cromer was used to dealing with Ethiopians. He was, as his father for thirty years had been before him, agent for the financial affairs of the Ethiopian royal family, and was in large measure responsible for the former Emperor's stupendous wealth. Now that Selassie was dead, Cromer still had regular contact with the family. He had been forced to explain several times to hopeful children, grandchildren, nephews

11

and nieces why it was not possible to release the substantial sums they claimed as their heritage. No will had been made, no instructions received. Funds could only be released against the Emperor's specific orders. In the event, the bank would of course administer the fortune, but was otherwise power-less to help . . .

So it wasn't the nationality that disturbed Cromer. It was the man's political background. Yufru came from the Embassy and hence, apparently, from the Marxist government that had destroyed Selassie. He guessed, therefore, that Yufru would have instructions to seek access to the Imperial fortune.

It was certainly a fortune worth having, as Cromer had known since childhood, for the connections between Selassie and Cromer's Bank went back over fifty years.

The story was an odd one, of considerable interest to historians of City affairs. Cromer's Bank had become a subsidiary of Rothschild's, the greatest bank of the day, in 1890. The link between Cromer's Bank and the Ethiopian royal family was established in 1924, when Ras Tafari, the future Haile Selassie, then Regent and heir to the throne, arrived in London, thus becoming the first Ethiopian ruler to travel abroad since the Queen of Sheba – whom Selassie claimed as his direct ancestor – visited Solomon.

Ras Tafari had several aims. Politically, he intended to drag his medieval country into the twentieth century. But his major concerns were personal and financial. As heir to the throne, he had access to wealth on a scale few can now truly comprehend, and he needed a safer home for it than the Imperial Treasure Houses in Addis Ababa and Axum.

Ethiopia's output of gold has never been known for sure, but was probably several tens of thousands of ounces annu-ally – in the nineteenth century at least. Ethiopia's mines, whose very location was a state secret, had for centuries been under direct Imperial control. Traditionally, the Emperor received one-third of the product, but the distinction between the state's funds and Imperial funds was somewhat academic. When Ras Tafari, resourceful, ambitious, wary of his rival princes, became heir, he inherited a quantity of gold estimated at some ten million ounces. He brought with him to London five million of those ounces – over 100 tons. By 1975 that gold was worth $800 million.

In London, Ras Tafari, who at that time spoke little English, discovered that the world's most reputable bank, Rothschild's, had a subsidiary named after a Cromer. By chance, the name meant a good deal to Selassie, for the Earl of Cromer, Evelyn Baring, had been governor general of the Sudan, Ethiopia's neighbour, in the early years of the century. It was of course pure coincidence, for Cromer the man had no connection with Cromer the title. Nevertheless, it clinched matters. Selassie placed most of his wealth in the hands of Sir Charles Cromer II, who had inherited the bank in 1911.

When Ras Tafari became Emperor in 1930 as Haile Selassie, the hoard was growing at the rate of 100,000 ounces per year. In 1935, when the Italians invaded, gold production ceased. The invasion drove Selassie into exile in Bath. There he chose to live in austerity to underline his role as the plucky victim of Fascist aggression. But he still kept a sharp eye on his deposits.

After his triumphant return, with British help, in 1941, gold production resumed. The British exchange agreements for 1944 and 1945 show that some 8000 ounces per month were exported from Ethiopia. A good deal more left unofficially. One estimate places Ethiopia's – or Selassie's – gold exports for 1941–74 at 200,000 ounces per annum.

This hoard was increased in the 1940s by a currency reform that removed from circulation in Ethiopia several million of the local coins, Maria Theresa silver dollars (which in the 1970s were still accepted as legal currency in remote parts of Ethiopia and elsewhere in the Middle East). Most of the coins were transferred abroad and placed in the Emperor's accounts. In 1975 Maria Theresa dollars had a market value of US$3.75 each.

In the 1950s, on the advice of young Charles Cromer himself, now heir to his aged father, Selassie's wealth was diversified. Investments were made on Wall Street and in a number of American companies, a policy intensified by Charles Cromer III after he took over in 1955, at the age of thirty-one.

By the mid-1970s Selassie's total wealth exceeded $2500 million.

Sir Charles knew that the fortune was secure, and that, with Selassie dead, his bank in particular, and those of his colleagues in Switzerland and New York, could continue to profit from the rising value of the gold indefinitely. The new government must know that there was no pressure that could be brought to bear to prise open the Emperor's coffers.

Why then, the visit?

There came a gentle buzz over the intercom.

Cromer leaned over, flicked a switch and said gently: 'Yes, Miss Yates?'

'Mr Yufru is here to see you, Sir Charles.'

'Excellent, excellent.' Cromer always took care to ensure that a new visitor, forming his first impressions, heard a tone that was soft, cultured and with just a hint of flattery. 'Please show Mr Yufru straight in.'

* * *

Six miles east of the City, in the suburban sprawl of east London, in one of a terrace of drab, two-up, two-down houses, two men sat at a table in a front room, the curtains drawn.

On the table stood an opened loaf of white sliced bread, some Cheddar, margarine, a jar of pickled onions and four cans of Guinness. One of the men was slim, jaunty, with a fizz of blond, curly hair and steady blue eyes. His name was Peter Halloran. He was wearing jeans, a pair of ancient track shoes and a denim jacket. In the corner stood his rucksack, into which was tucked an anorak. The other man, Frank Ridger, was older, with short, greying, curly hair, a bulbous nose and a hangdog mouth. He wore dungarees over a dirty check shirt.

They had been talking for an hour, since the surreptitious arrival of Halloran, who was now speaking. He dominated the conversation in a bantering Irish brogue, reciting the events of his life – the impatience at the poverty and dullness of village life in County Down, the decision to volunteer, the obsession with fitness, the love of danger, the successful application to join the SAS, anti-terrorist work in Aden in the mid-1960s and Oman (1971–4), and finally the return to Northern Ireland. It was all told with bravado and a surface glitter of which the older man was beginning to tire.

'Jesus, Frank,' the young man was saying, 'the Irish frighten me to death sometimes. I was in Mulligan's Bar in Dundalk, a quiet corner, me and a pint and a fellow named McHenry. I says to him there's a job. That's all I said. No details. I was getting to that, but not a bit of it – he didn't ask who, or what, or how much, or how do I get away? You know what he said? "When do I get the gun?" That's all he cared about. He didn't even care which *side* – MI5, the Provos, the Officials, the Garda. I liked that.'

'Well, Peter,' said Ridger. He spoke slowly. 'Did you do the job?'

'We did. You should've seen the papers. "IRA seize half a million in bank raid."'

'But,' said Ridger, draining his can, 'I thought you said you were paid by the Brits?'

'That's right,' said Halloran. He was enjoying playing the older man along, stoking his curiosity.

'The British paid you to rob a British bank?'

'That's right.'

'Were you back in favour or what?'

'After what happened in Oman? No way.'

'What did you do?'

'There was a girl.'

'Oh?'

'How was I to know who she was? I was on my way home for a couple of months' break. End of a contract. We had to get out or we'd have raped the camels. The lads, Mike Rourke among them, decided on a nice meal at the Sultan's new hotel, the Al Falajh. She was – what? Nineteen. Old enough. I tell you, Frank – shall I tell you, my son?'

Ridger grinned.

Halloran first saw her in the entrance hall. Lovely place, the Al Falajh. Velvet all over the shop. Like walking into an upmarket strip club. She was saying goodnight to Daddy, a visiting businessman, Halloran assumed. 'Go on then,' Rourke had said, seeing the direction of his glance. He slipped into the lift behind her. She was wearing a blouse, short-sleeved and loose, so that as she stood facing away from him, raising her slim arm to push the lift button, he could see that she was wearing a silk bra, and that it was quite unnecessary for her to wear a bra at all. He felt she should know this, and at once appointed himself her fashion adviser.

'Excuse me, miss, but I believe we have met.' He paused as she turned, with a half smile, eager to be polite.

He saw a tiny puzzle cloud her brow.

'Last night,' he said.

She frowned. 'I was . . .'

'In a fantasy,' he interrupted. It was corny, but it worked. By then she had been staring at him for seconds, and didn't know how to cut him. She smiled. Her name was Amanda Price-Whyckham.

'Eager as sin, she was,' Halloran went on. A most receptive student, was Amanda P-W. The only thing she knew was la-di-da. Never had a bit of rough, let alone a bit of Irish rough. So when Halloran admired the view as the light poured through the hotel window, and through her skirt, and suggested that simplicity was the thing – perhaps the necklace off, then the stockings, she agreed she looked better and better the less she wore. 'Until there she was, naked, and willing.' Halloran finished. 'My knees and elbows were raw by three in the morning.'

He smiled and took a swig of beer.

'I don't know how Daddy found out,' Halloran continued after a pause. 'Turned out he was a colonel on a visit for the MoD to see about some arms for the Omanis. You know, the famous Irish sheikhs – the O'Mahoneys?'

Ridger acknowledged the joke with a nod and a lugubrious smile.

'So Daddy had me out of there. The SAS didn't want me back, and I'd had enough of regular service. Used up half my salary to buy myself out. So it was back to pulling pints. Until the Brits approached me, unofficial like. Could I help discredit the Provos? Five hundred a month, in cash, for three months to see how it went. That was when my mind turned to banks.

It was easy – home ground, see, because we used to plan raids with the regiment. Just *plan* mind. Now it was for real. I got a taste for it. Next I know, the Garda's got me on file, and asks my controller in Belfast to have me arrested. He explains it nicely. They couldn't exactly come clean. So they do the decent thing: put out a warrant for me, but warn me first. Decent! You help your fucking country, and they fuck you.'

'You could tell.'

'I wouldn't survive to tell, Frank. As the bastard captain said, I'm OK if I lie low. In a year, two years, when the heat's off, I can live again.'

'I have the afternoon shift,' said Frank, avoiding his gaze, and standing up. 'I'll be back about nine.'

'We'll have a few drinks.'

As the door closed, Halloran reached for another can of Guinness. He had no intention of waiting even a week, let alone a year, to live again.

Yufru was clearly at ease in the cold opulence of Sir Charles Cromer's office. He was slim, with the aquiline good looks of many Ethiopians. He carried a grey cashmere overcoat, which he handed to Miss Yates, and wore a matching grey suit, tailored light-blue shirt and plain dark-blue tie.

Though Cromer never knew his background, Yufru had been living in exile since 1960. At that time he had been a major, a product of the elitist military academy at Harar. He had been one of a group of four officers who had determined to break the monolithic, self-seeking power of the monarchy and attempted to seize power while the Emperor was on a state visit to Brazil. The attempt was a disaster: the rebel officers, themselves arrogant and remote, never established how much support they would have, either within the army or outside it.

In the event, they had none. They took the entire cabinet hostage, shot most of them in an attempt to force the army into co-operation, and when they saw failure staring them in the face, scattered. Two killed themselves. Their corpses were strung up on a gallows in the centre of Addis. A third was captured and hanged. The fourth was Yufru. He drove over the border into Kenya, where he had been wise enough to bank his income, and surfaced a year later in London. Now, after a decade in business, mainly handling African art and supervising the investment of his profits, he had volunteered his services to the revolutionary government, seeking some revenge on the Imperial family and rightly guessing that his experience of the capitalist system might be of use.

He stood and looked round with admiration. Then, as Cromer invited him with a gesture to sit, he began to speak in suave tones that were the consequence of service with the British in 1941-5.

As Cromer knew, Ethiopia was a poor country. He, Yufru, had been lucky, of course, but the time had come for all of them to pull together. They faced the consequences of a terrible famine. The figures quoted in the West were not inaccurate – perhaps half a million would eventually die of starvation. Much, of course, was due to the inhumanity of the Emperor. He was remote, cut off in his palaces. The revolutionary government had attempted to reverse these disasters, but there was a limit imposed by a lack of funds and internal opposition.

'These are difficult times politically,' Yufru sighed. He was the ideal apologist for his thuggish masters. Cromer had met the type before – intelligent, educated, smooth, serving themselves by serving the hand that paid them. 'We have enemies within who will soon be persuaded to see the necessity of change. We have foolish rebels in Eritrea who may seek to dismember our country. Somalia wishes to tear from us the Ogaden, an integral part of our country.

'All this demands a number of extremely expensive operations. As you are no doubt aware, the Somalis are well equipped with Soviet arms. My government has not as yet found favour with the Soviets. If we are to be secure – and I suggest that it is in the interests of the West that the Horn of Africa remains stable – we need good, modern arms. The only possible source at present is the West. We do not wish to be a debtor nation. We would like to buy.

'For that, to put matters bluntly, we need hard cash.'

Cromer nodded. He had guessed correctly.

'The money for such purposes exists. It was stolen by Haile Selassie from our people and removed from the country, as you have good cause to know. I am sure you will respect the fact that the Emperor's fortune is officially government property and that the people of Ethiopia, the originators of that wealth, should be considered the true heirs of the Emperor. They should receive the benefits of their labours.'

'Administered, of course, by your government,' Cromer put in.

'Of course,' Yufru replied easily, untouched by the banker's irony. 'They are the representatives of the people.'

Cromer was in his element. He knew his ground and he knew it to be rock-solid. He could afford to be magnanimous.

'Mr Yufru,' he began after a pause, 'morally your arguments are impeccable. I understand the fervour with which your government is determined to right historic wrongs . . .' – both of them were aware of what the fervour entailed: hundreds of corpses, 'enemies of the revolution', stinking on the streets of Addis – 'and we would naturally be willing to help in any way. But insofar as the Emperor's personal funds

20

are concerned, there is really nothing we can do. Our instructions are clear and binding . . .'

'I too know the instructions,' Yufru broke in icily. 'My father was with the Emperor in '24. That is, in part, why I am here. You must have written instructions, signed by the Emperor, and sealed with the Imperial seal, on notepaper prepared by your bank, itself watermarked, again with the Imperial seal.'

Cromer acknowledged Yufru's assertion with a slow nod.

'Indeed, and those arrangements still stand. I have to tell you that the last such communication received by this bank was dated July 1974. Neither I nor my associates have received any further communication. We cannot take any action unilaterally. And, as the world knows, the Emperor is now dead, and it seems that the deposits must be frozen . . .' – the banker spread his hands in a gesture of resigned sympathy – 'in perpetuity.'

There was a long pause. Yufru clearly had something else to say. Cromer waited, still confident.

'Sir Charles,' Yufru said, more carefully now, 'we have much work to do to regularize the Imperial records. The business of fifty years, you understand . . . It may be that the Emperor has left among his papers further instructions, perhaps written in the course of the revolution itself. And he was alive, you will remember, for a year after the revolution. It is conceivable that other papers relating to his finances will emerge. I take it that there would be no question that your bank and your associated banks would accept such instructions, if properly authenticated?'

The sly little bastard – he's got something up his sleeve, thought Cromer. It may be . . . it is conceivable . . . if, if, if. There was no 'if' about it. Something solid lay behind the question.

To gain time he said: 'I will have to check my own arrangements and those of my colleagues . . . there is something about outdated instructions which slips my mind. Anyway,' he hastened on, 'the instructions have always involved either new deposits or the transfer of funds and the buying of metals or stock. In what way would you have an interest in transmitting such information?'

Yufru replied, evenly: 'We would like to be correct. We would merely like to be aware of your reactions if such papers were found and if we decided to pursue the matter.'

'It seems an unlikely contingency, Mr Yufru. The Emperor has, after all, been dead six months.'

'We are, of course, talking hypothetically, Sir Charles. We simply wish to be prepared.' He rose, and removed a speck from his jacket. 'Now, I must leave you to consider my question. May I thank you for your excellent coffee and your advice. Until next time, then.'

Puzzled, Sir Charles showed Yufru to the door. He was not a little apprehensive. There was something afoot. Yufru's bosses were not noted for their philanthropy. They would have no interest in passing on instructions that might increase the Emperor's funds.

It made no sense.

But by tonight, it damn well would.

'No calls, Miss Yates,' he said abruptly into the intercom. 'And bring me the correspondence files for Lion . . . Yes, all of them. The whole damn filing cabinet.'

That evening, Sir Charles sat alone till late. A set of files lay on his desk. Against the wall stood the cabinet of files relating to Selassie. He again reviewed his thoughts on Yufru's visit. He had to assume that there was something behind it. The only idea that made any sense was that there was some scheme to wrest Selassie's money from the banks concerned. It couldn't be done by halves. If they had access – with forged papers, say – then he had to assume that the whole lot was at risk.

And what a risk. He let his mind explore that possibility. Two thousand million dollars' worth of gold from three countries for a start. If he were instructed, as it were by the Emperor himself, to sell every last ounce, it would be a severe blow to the liquidity of his own bank and those of his partners in Zurich and New York. With capital withdrawn, loans would have to be curtailed, profits lost. When and if it became known who was selling, reputations would suffer and rumours spread. Confidence would be lost. Even if there weren't panic withdrawals, future deposits would be withheld. The effects would echo down the years and along the corridors of financial power, spreading chaos. With that much gold unloaded all at once, the price would tumble. And not only would he fail to realize the true market value, but he would become a pariah within Rothschild's and in the international banking community. Cromer's, renowned for its discretion, would be front-page news.

And that was just the gold. There would be the winding-up of a score of companies, the withdrawal of the cash balances, in sterling, Swiss francs and dollars.

Good God, he would be a liability. *Eased out.*

He poured himself a whisky and returned to his desk, forcing himself to consider the worst. In what circumstances might such a disaster occur?

What if Yufru produced documents bearing the Emperor's signature, ordering his estate to be handed over to Mengistu's bunch? With any luck they would be forgeries and easily spotted. On the other hand, they might be genuine, dating from before the Emperor's death. But that was surely beyond the bounds of possibility. It would belie everything he knew about the man – ruthless, uncompromising, implacably opposed to any diminution of his authority.

But what if they had got at him, with drugs, or torture or solitary confinement? Now that was a possibility. Cromer would gamble his life on it that Selassie had signed nothing to prejudice his personal fortune before he was overthrown. But he might have done afterwards, if forced. He had after all been in confinement for about a year.

Now he had faced the implications, however, he saw that he could forestall the very possibility Yufru had mentioned. He checked one of the files before him again. Yes, no documents signed by the Emperor would be acceptable after such a delay. Anyone receiving written orders more than two weeks old had to check back on the current validity of those orders before acting upon them. The device was a sensible precaution in the days when couriers were less reliable than now, and communications less rapid. The action outlined in that particular clause had never been taken, and the clause never revoked. There it still stood, Cromer's bastion against hypothetical catastrophe.

Cromer relaxed. But before long he began to feel resentful that he had wasted an evening on such a remote eventuality. He downed his whisky, turned off his lights, strolled over to the lift and descended to the basement, where the Daimler awaited him, his chauffeur dozing gently at the wheel. He was at his London home by midnight.

Friday 19 March
'So you see, Mr Yufru, how my colleagues and I feel.'

Cromer had summoned Yufru for a further meeting earlier that morning.

'After such a lapse of time and given the uncertainty of the political situation, we could not be certain that the documents would represent the Emperor's lasting and final wishes. We would be required to seek additional confirmation, at source, before taking action. And the source, of course, is no longer with us.'

'I see, Sir Charles. You would not, however, doubt the validity of the Emperor's signature and seal?'

'No, indeed. That we can authenticate.'

'You would merely doubt the validity of his wishes, given the age of the documents?'

'That is correct.'

'I see. In that case, I am sure such a problem will never arise.'

Cromer nodded. The whole ridiculous, explosive scheme – if it had ever existed outside his own racing imagination – had been scotched. And apparently with no complications.

To hear Yufru talk, one would think the whole thing was indeed a mere hypothesis. Yufru remained affable, passed some complimentary comments about Cromer's taste, and left, in relaxed mood.

The banker remained at his desk, deep in thought. He had no immediate appointments before lunch with a broker at 12.30, and he had the nagging feeling that he had missed something. There were surely only two possibilities. Mengistu's bunch might have forged, or considered forging, documents. Or they might have the genuine article, however obtained. In either case, the date would precede Selassie's death and they would now know that the date alone would automatically make the orders unacceptable. The fortune would remain for ever out of their reach.

Yufru had failed. Or had he? He didn't seem like a man who had failed – not angry, or depressed, or fearful at reporting what

25

might be a serious setback to the hopes of his masters. No: it was more as if he had merely ruled out just one course of action.

What other course remained open? What had he, Cromer, said that allowed the Ethiopians any freedom of action? The only positive statement he had made was that the orders, if they followed procedure, would be accepted as genuine documents, even if outdated.

Under what circumstances would the orders be accepted both as genuine and binding? If the date was recent, of course, but then . . . If the date was recent . . . in that case the Emperor would have to be . . . Dear God!

Cromer sat bolt upright, staring, unseeing, across the room. He had experienced what has been called the Eureka effect: a revelation based on the most tenuous evidence, but of such power that the conclusion is undeniable.

The Emperor must still be alive.

Cromer sat horrified at his own realization. He had no real doubts about his conclusion. It was the only theory that made sense out of Yufru's approach. But he had to be certain that there was nothing to contradict it.

From the cabinet, against the wall, he slid out a file marked 'Clippings – Death'. There, neatly tabbed into a loose-leaf folder, were a number of reports of Selassie's death, announced on 28 August 1975 as having occurred the previous day, in his sleep, aged eighty-three.

According to the official government hand-out: 'The Emperor complained of feeling unwell the previous night (26 August) but a doctor could not be obtained and a servant found him dead the next morning.'

Although he had been kept under close arrest in the compound in the Menelik Palace, there was no suggestion that he had been ailing. True, he had had a prostate operation two months before, but he had recovered well. One English doctor who treated him at that time, a professor from Queen Mary's Hospital, London, was quoted as saying he had 'never seen a patient of that age take the operation better'.

There had never been any further details. No family member was allowed to see the body. There was no post-mortem. The burial, supposedly on 29 August, was secret. There was no funeral service. The Emperor had, to all intents and purposes, simply vanished.

Not unnaturally, a number of people, in particular Selassie's family, found the official account totally unacceptable. It reeked of duplicity. However disruptive the revolution, there were scores of doctors in Addis Ababa. Rumours began to circulate that Selassie had been smothered, murdered to ease the task of the revolution, for all the while he was known to be alive, large sections of the population would continue to regard him, even worship him, as the true ruler of the country. As *The Times* said when reporting the family's opinion in June 1976: 'The Emperor's sudden death has always caused suspicion, if only because of the complete absence of medical or legal authority for the way he died.'

And so the matter rested. Until now. No wonder there had been no medical or legal authority for the way he died, mused Cromer. But the family had jumped to the wrong conclusion.

'Sir Charles,' it was Miss Yates's voice on the intercom. 'Will you be lunching with Sir Geoffrey after all?'

'Ah, Miss Yates, thank you. Yes. Tell him I'm on my way. Be there in ten minutes.'

He stopped at the desk on his way out.

'What appointments are there this afternoon?' he asked.

'You have a meeting with Mr Squires at two o'clock about the Shah's most recent deposits. And of course the usual gold committee meeting at five.'

The Shah could wait. 'Cancel Jeremy. I need the early afternoon clear.'

He glanced out of the window. It looked like rain. He took one of the two silk umbrellas from beside Valerie's desk and left for lunch.

2

Those who had met Sir Charles Cromer over the past twenty years knew him only as a calculating financier, who seemed to live for his bank, seeking a release in his work from a stultifying home life. In point of fact, he was a closet gangster, utterly amoral, and with more than a dash of sadism in him. This aspect of his character had long been suppressed by his intelligence, his social standing and the eminence of the professional role he had inherited.

Only twice in his life had Cromer truly expressed himself. The first time was at school, at Eton. There, as fag and junior, he had borne the crushing humiliations imposed upon him by his seniors, knowing that he too would one day inherit their power. His resilience and forbearance were well rewarded. He became a games player of some eminence, playing scrum-half for the school and for Hereford Schoolboys with a legendary fearlessness. He also became Head of House. In this capacity he had cause, about once a week, to dispense discipline in the sternest public school traditions. Sometimes he would preside, with awful formality, over the ritual humiliation of some unfortunate junior who would be beaten in the prefects' common room. Meanwhile the prefects themselves read idly, disdainfully refusing to acknowledge the presence of the abhorrent object of Cromer's displeasure. Sometimes, for a lesser offence, the beating would be administered in his own study. Both occasions gave him joy.

It was at a House beating in his own study that he once allowed his nature to get the better of him. The boy concerned had dared question the validity of his decision. The insolence of the suggestion drove the eighteen-year-old Cromer into a cold and dedicated anger. The beating he then delivered, with the full weight of his body, drew blood beneath the younger boy's trousers. When examined by a doctor, marks were even found on the victim's groin, where the cane had whipped around the side of his buttock and hip.

The traditions of the school demanded complete stoicism. Even after such a caning, the boy would have been expected to shake hands with his persecutor, then continue life as normal. He might bear the stigmata for weeks, but he would say nothing, nor would anybody else.

This time, however, there was a comeback. The boy's father was a Jewish textile manufacturer determined to buy the trappings of English culture for his offspring. The boy himself was less certain that he needed them. Cromer's actions decided him: he telephoned his father, who appeared the following day, pulled his son out of school and obtained a doctor's report. Copies of the report were passed to the headmaster, the housemaster, Cromer's parents and his own solicitor. It was only with the greatest skill that a public scandal was averted. Cromer himself, who was amazed to find that he was considered to have done something amiss, was severely reprimanded. It changed his attitude not at all. But it did teach him that, if he wished to indulge in such activities, he would have to cloak them in a veneer of respectability.

The only other time that Cromer was able to let himself go was in Berlin immediately after the war. He had been too young to see any active service. The war was over just as he finished his training. As a newly commissioned second lieutenant, he flew into Tempelhof airport in Berlin in July 1945, the first time the victorious Russians had allowed the Western allies into the former German capital. Berlin was still a charnel house, a wilderness of buildings torn apart, squares and streets littered with rubble, a population half-starved. Cromer rapidly saw that he had been presented with a unique opportunity. The occupying troops were the élite, buying goods, labour and sex with money, cigarettes, food, luxury goods. Marks were worth nothing; sterling and dollars were like gold.

For the first year, when the Germans were still regarded as the enemy and the Russians as friends, Cromer was in his element. He transferred in his own cash and bought for derisory sums anything of value he could lay his hands on. It was amazing that so much had survived the war unscathed – Meissen china, Steinway and Bechstein grand pianos, hall-marked silver, exquisitely embroidered linen, nineteenth-century military paraphernalia by the ton, even a Rolls-Royce Silver Ghost. He hired a warehouse near Tempelhof and had it sealed off. For two years, he packed in his treasures. He was by no means the only one to take advantage of the Berliners in this way, though in the scale of his operations he was practically unique.

In early 1948 Cromer, now a captain, was given as administrative assistant a teenage second lieutenant, Richard Collins. For Cromer, this turned out to be a providential appointment. As well as fulfilling his normal duties, organizing patrols and the distribution of food, Collins was soon recruited after hours to supervise the stowing of Cromer's latest acquisitions.

31

It was not a demanding job – a couple of evenings a week at most – but it was regular, and he was promised a share of the proceeds.

One evening in May, when Collins was closing up for the night, a task he had been taught to do surreptitiously, he heard a crash around the corner. He ran to the side of the building and was in time to see a bottle, flaming at one end, sail through the newly made hole in one of the windows. A Molotov cocktail.

Collins knew it would be caught by the wire-mesh netting inside the window and guessed it would do little damage. Hardly pausing, he sprinted into the rubble-strewn shadows from which the bottle had come, in time to see a slight figure vanishing round the next street corner. Collins was young, fit and well fed, and the teenage fire-bug, weakened by years of malnutrition, had no chance of escape. Collins sprinted up from behind and pushed him hard in the shoulders. The German took off forwards into a heap of rubble, hit it head on and collapsed into the bricks like a sack of potatoes. Collins hauled him over, and found his head dreadfully gashed and his neck broken.

Collins heaved the body across the unlit street and into a bombed building. He then ran back to the warehouse, retrieved the guttering, still unbroken bottle of petrol from the wire grill, stamped out the cloth, poured the contents down a drain, slung the bottle away into the roadside rubble, listened to see if the crash and the noise of running feet would bring a patrol, and then, reassured, went off to find Cromer.

Cromer knew what he owed Collins. He used his own jeep to pick up the body, and by three o'clock in the morning the German had become just another unidentified corpse in a small canal.

There had been some mention of German resentment against profiteering, but this was the first direct evidence Cromer had had of it. He saw that the time had come to stop.

Within a couple of months, Berlin was blockaded by the Russians and the airlift was under way. Planes loaded with food and fuel from the West were landing at Tempelhof every three minutes and taking off again, empty. Except that some were not empty. It took Cromer only two weeks to organize the shipment of his complete stock in twin-engine Dakotas, first to Fassberg, then on to England, to a hangar on a Midlands service aerodrome. A year later, demobbed, Cromer organized two massive auctions that netted him £150,000. In Berlin his outlay had been just £17,000. Not bad for a twenty-four-year-old with no business experience and no more than a small allowance from the business he was destined to take over.

Now Cromer the racketeer was about to resurface.

After lunch Cromer returned temporarily to his hermit-like existence. His staff did not find his behaviour peculiar; there had been crises demanding his personal attention before. He made two telephone calls. The first was to Oswald Kupferbach in Zurich, to an office in the Crédit Suisse, 8 Paradeplatz – one of the few banks in Switzerland which have special telephone and telex lines solely for dealing in gold bullion.

'Oswald? *Wie geht's dir?* . . . Yes, a long time. We have to meet as soon as possible . . . I'm afraid so. Something has come up over here. It's about Lion . . . Yes, it's serious, but not over the phone. You have to be here . . . I can only say that it concerns all our futures very closely . . . Ideally, this weekend? Sunday evening for Monday morning? That would be perfect . . . You and Jerry . . . I'll have a car for you and a hotel. I'll telex the details.'

The next call was to New York, to a small bank off Wall Street that had specialities comparable to Cromer's – though little gold, of course, and more stock-exchange dealings – and a relationship with the Morgan Guaranty Trust Company similar to Cromer's with Rothschild's. He spoke to Jerry Lodge.

'Jerry? Charlie. It's about Lion . . .'

The call had a similar pattern to the previous one – prevarication from the other end, further persuasion by Cromer, mention of mutual futures at stake and, finally, a meeting arranged for Monday morning.

In an elegant courtyard of Cotswold-stone farm buildings, some seventy miles north-west of London, Richard Collins raised an arm in a perfunctory farewell to a customer driving off in a Land Rover. A routine morning's work. One down, twenty-five to go, a job lot from Leyland.

A lot of people envied Dicky Collins. He looked the very epitome of the well-to-do countryman in his tweed jackets, twill trousers, Barbour coats. His Range Rover had a Blaupunkt tape deck, still something of a rarity in the mid-1970s. The farmhouse, with its courtyard and outbuildings, was surrounded by ten acres of woodland and meadow. It was an ideal base for his business, which was mainly selling army-surplus vehicles. In one of the stone barns, converted into a full working garage, there were five Second World War jeeps in various stages of repair, a khaki truck that had last seen action in the Western desert, and several 1930s motorbikes, still with side-cars.

The business turned over quarter of a million. He took £25,000, more than enough in those days. He was forty-eight, fit, successful, unmarried, and bored out of his bloody mind.

For almost ten years he had worked at his bloody Land Rovers and jeeps and trucks, ever since he finished in Aden and Charlie Cromer had given him a £100,000 loan to buy his first 100 vehicles – in exchange for sixty per cent of the equity. Both had judged well. It was a good business, doing the rounds of the War Department auctions. Now things were drying up, prices were rising. Any old jeep you could have got for £100 ten years before now fetched £2000 and up. It was a specialist field, and Collins knew it well. Once he had loved it. The sweet purr of a newly restored engine reminded him of the real thing.

After Aden, he was happy to settle. Hell of a time. Fuzzies fighting for a stump of a country and an oven of a city. Chap needed two gallons of water a day just to stay alive. No point to it all in the end, with Britain pulling out. Not like Borneo – that had been a proper show, all the training put to good use.

Now he was sick of it. Country life could never deliver that sort of kick. Money? It was good, but it would never be enough to excite him. The place was mortgaged to the hilt, the taxman was a sadist, and even if he sold, Charlie Cromer would take most of the profits.

Boredom, that was Collins's problem. There was old Molly to do the house. The business ran itself these days, what with Caroline coming in two days a week to keep the VAT man at bay. Stan knew all about a car's innards and could fix anything over twenty years old as good as new. Collins had other interests, of course, but keeping up with publications on international terrorism and his thrice-weekly clay-pigeon practices hardly compared with jungle warfare for thrills. There were parties, there were girls for the asking, but he wasn't about to marry again. What had once been a comfortable country nest had become a padded cell.

'Major,' Stan called from the garage. 'Phone.'

Collins nodded. He walked through the garage, edging his way past a skeletal jeep to the phone.

'Dicky? Charlie Cromer. Got a proposition for you.'

Monday, 22 March

That morning, Sir Charles Cromer, Oswald Kupferbach and Jerry Lodge were together in Cromer's office. The Swiss and the American sat facing each other on the Moroccan leather sofas beneath the Modigliani. Both had been chosen for their present jobs only after an interview with Cromer, who had judged them right for his needs: astute, experienced, hard. Kupferbach, fifty-two, with rimless glasses, had practised discretion for so long he never seemed to have any emotions at all. Professionally, he didn't. His one passion was personal: he was an expert in the ecology of mountains above the tree line. Lodge – his grandparents were Poles from the city of Lodz – was quite a contrast: bluff, rotund, reassuring. He found it easy to ensure he was underestimated by rivals.

Between the two on the glass-topped table was newly made coffee and orange juice. Sir Charles was standing, coffee cup in hand, having just outlined the approaches made to him by Yufru.

He concluded by saying: 'So you see, gentlemen, why we had to meet: I have the strongest possible reasons for believing that the Emperor is not dead. I further believe that unless we move rapidly and in concert, we shall shortly be presented with documents bearing the Emperor's signature demanding the release of his fortune to the revolutionary government of Mengistu Haile Mariam.

'This would be a financial blow that we, as individual bankers, should not have to endure. Indeed, the sums in gold alone are so vast that their release would devastate the world's gold markets. While the short-term implications for our respective economies are not pleasant, the implications for our banks and ourselves as individuals are horrendous.'

The Swiss was thoughtful, the American wide-eyed, caricaturing disbelief.

'Oh, come on, Charlie,' he said, 'that's got to be the most outrageous proposition I've ever heard. What are you on? I mean, my God.'

Kupferbach broke in: 'No, no, Jerry. It is not so foolish. It fits in. There have been a number of approaches in Zurich for loans. They need the money. But their propositions are unrealistic. The World Bank might consider a loan for fighting the famine, but, of course, it would be administered by World Bank officials. They don't want that.'

Lodge paused. 'OK, OK,' he said at last, 'let's follow it through. Suppose the old boy is still alive. Suppose he signs the papers. Don't you think we could persuade the Ethiopians to leave the gold with us? After all, they have to place it somewhere, don't they? We arrange a loan for them based on the reserves. They buy their arms and fight their goddam wars, and everyone's happy. Hey?'

'It's possible,' Cromer said slowly, 'but it doesn't look like a safe bet to me. You think Mengistu would pay interest, and if he did, do you think his successors would? Would you invest in a Marxist without any experience of international finance who came to power and preserves power through violence?'

'I agree. But what do you think would happen if we received these documents and simply ignored them?' replied Kupferbach.

'Whadya mean, Ozzie?' said Lodge. 'We just don't do as we're told? We say we're not going to hand over the funds? We tell the Ethiopians to go stuff their asses?'

37

'In brief, *meine Herren* yes.'

'If all this is true,' said Cromer, 'that thought must have already crossed their minds. In their position, what would your answer be?'

'Right,' Lodge said, jutting his lower jaw and biting his top lip. 'Jesus, if I was them, I'd make one hell of a storm. Major banks refusing to honour their obligations? Yeah, they could really have a go at us. International Court at The Hague, questions in the UN, pressure on other African countries to make holes in Rothschild and Morgan Guaranty investments in the Third World. We'd come out of it with more than egg on our faces.'

'Of course,' added Cromer, 'to do that, they'd have to reveal that Selassie was still alive. It would make them look pretty damn stupid.'

'Yes, but they have less to lose.' It was Kupferbach again, a clear thinker with a coolness that more than matched Cromer's. 'Mengistu could write off the previous announcement of the Emperor's death as a necessity imposed by the revolution. The publicity would be bad for them, but could be catastrophic for us.'

Cromer looked at the two of them in turn.

'Gentlemen,' he said, 'I have been thinking of nothing else for the last two days. I have rehearsed these arguments many times in my own mind. If the Emperor signs those papers we are lost.' He paused. 'We are left with no choice – we have to assume the Emperor is still alive, and we have to get to him before he signs anything.'

Cromer's two colleagues looked at him expectantly.

'What the hell are you suggesting?' said Lodge.

'We have to do the decent thing. We have to kidnap the Emperor.'

They stared at him.

Lodge shook his head in disbelief and went on shaking it, perhaps at the very suggestion, or perhaps at the impossibility of achieving it.

'Jerry, Oswald: don't fight it. It's the only answer. It's either that or immediate retirement. I don't know about you two but I have a very real future in front of me. The Emperor has none. Getting him out, we win all ways. We save him, and we save his fortune – and ours.'

'You goddam English,' said Lodge. 'You think you can still act like you had an Empire. Where I come from, the CIA do that sort of thing, not the goddam bankers . . .' He trailed off, still shaking his head.

Kupferbach seemed to be way ahead of him. 'I see, Charles. You have been doing much preparation for this meeting. May I ask, therefore, why you needed to include us?'

'For the first step, Oswald, the first step. Getting to Selassie. I think I know how to do it. We still have one card to play. Supposing he is still alive, supposing the Ethiopians make him sign the documents, supposing they are dated for just two days before we receive them, I still do not believe we would have to comply. We could argue that the signature must have been produced under duress, since it is clearly contrary to everything the Emperor has expressed in the past. I think we could make such a refusal stand up in a court of law. Of course, it would not do to let things go on that far. As you say, Oswald, the publicity would be catastrophic. But likewise, they would not get their money.

'I think we can pre-empt a crisis. We tell them that signature under duress would not be acceptable, quoting UN Human Rights legislation. I also think I could suggest a way around the difficulty: I will propose that the signature be made in the presence either of the bankers concerned or of their duly appointed representatives, in a situation in which the Emperor could be seen – for that particular day, at least – to be in good health and not the object of undue pressure, physical or psychological.

'That, gentlemen, is how we gain access.'

'Hold on there a tiny minute,' broke in Lodge, 'you're losing me. You mean this has to be done for real? We have to go and meet the Emperor?'

'Well, not we necessarily, but yes, there has to be a meeting between our people and the Emperor. And there are, of course, a number of other implications. The Emperor will have to be in a fit state to hold such a meeting. But then, presumably, he has to be in a fit state to sign the documents at all, so it shouldn't be too much of a problem to produce him in a reasonable state of health.

'A further implication – and this is where I need you – is that the documents for signature have to be genuine. Only in that way can we guarantee access. We have to see what the Ethiopians want from Selassie, and we have to agree to them in advance. And Selassie will agree.'

'Yeah?' said Lodge, sceptically. 'Tell me why.'

'One good reason – only with our co-operation can he assure the financial future of his family abroad. I've already had the family on my back several times. It is clear that, in a year or two, they will not be able to support themselves in the manner to which they have become accustomed. There are several children and countless grandchildren. All will need financial help, which they will not receive unless Selassie signs what will become, in effect, his last will and testament, one that must also be agreed with the Ethiopian government and ourselves. Everything must be prepared in secret, but as if it was for real.

'Thereafter, our duty to ourselves is clear: we cannot allow Selassie actually to sign the papers.'

Collins arrived in London early on Monday evening, parked his Range Rover in a garage off Berkeley Square and strolled round to Brown's hotel in Dover Street. He just had time for a bath, and a whisky and water in his room, when the internal phone went to announce the arrival in reception of Charlie Cromer.

The two dined at the Vendôme, where sole may be had in twenty-four different styles. It took Cromer two courses and most of a very dry Chablis to bring Collins up to date.

'And now,' he said over coffee, 'before I make you any propositions, I want to know how you're fixed. How's the business?'

'You've seen the books, even if you don't remember them. The profits are there. But there's a problem with the management.'

'Fire him.'

'It's *me*, Charlie. It was a joke.' Cromer shrugged an apology. 'I'm bored. I've been thinking about getting out, taking off somewhere for a year.'

'Not a woman, is it?'

'No. I have to keep my nose clean around home – get a reputation for dipping your wick and business can suffer.'

'So do I take it my call was timely?'

'Indeed.'

'Good. You can see what I need: a team of hit men, as our American friends say. We'll have to work out the details together, but, for a start, we need two more like you, men who like danger, who like a challenge, cool and experienced.'

'What are you offering in return?'

'To you? Freedom. I'll arrange a purchaser for the company and turn any profits over to you. I would imagine you will come out of it with, say, £100,000 in cash. In addition, $100,000 to be deposited in your name in New York and a similar sum to be placed in a numbered account in Switzerland.'

'That sounds generous.'

'Fair. I have colleagues who are interested in the successful outcome of this particular operation.'

Collins had decided to take up the offer in any case. 'Yes. I'm on. I still have a few contacts in the Regiment. I can think of a couple of chaps who may be interested.'

'There's another thing,' said Cromer. 'You will all have to act the part of bankers. For obvious reasons, I can't go. Wish I could.'

'No, you don't, Charlie. It's far too risky.'

'You'll be handing me a white feather next.'

'For *us*, Charlie. Kidnapping an Emperor is quite enough for one job. Spare us looking after you.'

Tuesday, 23 March
Back in the Oxfordshire countryside, Collins had only a few routine matters to attend to. He had to confirm a couple of sales, vet a US Army jeep that would eventually fetch at least £3500, and say 'yes' with a willing smile when the village's up-and-coming young equestrienne, Caroline Sinclair, wanted some poles for a jump. But most of his attention was given to tracking down Halloran and Rourke.

It took several calls and several hours to get to Halloran. He learned of Halloran's rapid exit from the SAS, and of his re-emergence in Ireland. A contact in Military Intelligence, Belfast, looked up the files. Halloran had blown it: he was never to be used again. For them, Halloran had turned out more dangerous than an unexploded bomb. There had been reprimands for taking him on in the first place. A couple of his Irish contacts were also on file.

'What's this for, old boy?' the voice at the end of the line asked. 'Nothing too fishy, I hope?'

Collins knew what this meant. 'Nothing to do with the Specials, the Army, the UDA, the IRA or the SAS. Something far, far away.'

'Good. In that case, you better move fast. The Yard knows he's in London. Looks like the Garda tipped them the wink. Could be a bit embarrassing for us if they handle it wrong. Do what you can.'

Collins made three more calls, this time to the Republic – one to a bar in Dundalk and one to each of the contacts on MI's file. At each number he left a message that an old friend was trying to contact Pete Halloran with an offer of work. He left his number.

At lunch-time, the phone rang. A call-box: the pips cut off as the money went in. A voice heavily muffled through a handkerchief asked for Collins's identity. Then: 'It's about Halloran.'

'I'll make it short,' said Collins. 'Tell Pete the Yard are on to him and that I may have an offer. Tell him to move quickly.'

'I'll let him know.'

The phone clicked off. It could have been Halloran, probably was, but he had to be allowed to handle things his own way.

An hour later, Halloran himself called.

'Is that you, sir? I had the message. What's the offer?'

'Good to hear you, Peter. Nothing definite yet. But I want you to stay out of trouble and be ready for a show. Not here – a long way away. You can come up here as soon as you like. You'll be quite safe.'

He had assumed Halloran, on the run, tense, perhaps bored with remaining hidden, would jump at it. He did.

'But what's this about the Yard?'

'Just a report that your name has been passed over. Are you sure your tracks are covered? Maybe nothing in it, but just look after yourself, will you? Phone again tomorrow at this time. Perhaps I'll have more.'

The second set of calls was simpler. From the SAS in Herefordshire to the Selous Scouts in Rhodesia was an easy link. He had no direct contact there, but didn't need one. He was told Rourke was on his way home. The call also elicited the address of Rourke's family – a suburban house in Sevenoaks, Kent. Rourke senior was still a working man, a British Rail traffic supervisor. Mrs Rourke answered. Oh yes, Michael was on his way home. Why, he might be in London at that very moment. No, they didn't know where. He liked his independence, did Michael. They hoped he would be down in the morning, but anyway he was certain to call. How nice of the major. Michael would be pleased to re-establish an old link. No, they didn't think he had any immediate plans. Yes, she would pass on the message.

Rourke phoned that afternoon within an hour of Halloran. He was still at Heathrow, just arrived from Jo'burg.

'Can't tell you yet, Michael,' said Collins, in response to Rourke's first question. 'But it looks like a bit of the old times. Lots of action, one-month contract. Can you be free?'

There was a pause. 'I'm interested.'

Again, Collins made a provisional arrangement. Rourke would be back in contact later that evening.

Collins's final call that afternoon, shortly before four o'clock, was to Cromer.

'Charlie. Just wanted to say the package we were lining up the other day looks good. The other two partners are very interested. We're ready when you give us the word.'

'Thanks, Dicky. I have a meeting later which should clarify things. I'll be in contact tonight.'

3

At five o'clock, with the business of the day cleared from his desk, Cromer prepared himself for Yufru's arrival. Valerie Yates was briefed to leave when she saw him. Cromer did not want the possibility of any eavesdropping, intentional or otherwise.

He had planned for himself the role he liked best – magnanimous, controlled, polite, manipulative. He did not wish to be overtly aggressive and thus risk forcing Yufru into a corner. If he had guessed correctly, it should be a delicate, but not difficult matter to persuade him that the two of them should be working together.

'Mr Yufru, Sir Charles,' came Valerie's voice over the intercom.

'Very good, Miss Yates, ask him to come in, and perhaps you could bring in some tea before you go . . . ah, Mr Yufru, I am sorry to impose upon your precious time. Shall we?' And he indicated the sofas.

'It is my pleasure, Sir Charles. Perhaps it is I that owe you an apology. I had no intention of involving you in such an extended intellectual exercise', said Yufru, as he relaxed back into the ancient polished leather. He crossed his right leg

47

over his left and set the crease of his grey trousers exactly over the kneecap.

'Your idea interested me,' Cromer said, 'so much so that I began to treat it less as an intellectual exercise and more as a practical possibility.'

Yufru's hands came to rest in his lap. He gave no hint of concern.

Cromer continued: 'That way, I can be sure that my response will be complete and therefore as helpful as possible. It is because I think I now finally have a realistic answer to your question that I wish to speak to you.'

Valerie knocked at the door and brought in a tray bearing two neat little porcelain cups, teapot, sugar bowl, teaspoons, milk jug and lemon. Yufru was now utterly still, his face expressionless, his attention riveted on Cromer. As Valerie set down the tray on the table between the two men he said smoothly: 'By all means let us cover all eventualities, Sir Charles.'

Cromer waited until Valerie had closed the door and resumed: 'In our previous conversation, Mr Yufru, we discussed the possibility of my bank being presented with documents signed by the Emperor several months ago. I said an outdated signature would not be acceptable. I think I should tell you that the date alone would not be our only reason for our refusal to comply with instructions.

'We are speaking of documents signed by the Emperor after his deposition. It is well known that he was not a free man. We have no reason to think he was badly treated; but equally we must assume, for our client's sake, that instructions not in his direct interest might have been the product of coercion. In other words, in the circumstances you outlined, we would have a justifiable fear that he might have been forced to append his signature to documents not of his own devising. I fear, therefore, that we could not accept the Emperor's instructions as both authentic and valid. The date, you see, would be irrelevant if the Emperor was a prisoner at the time of his signature.'

Yufru had begun to breathe a little quicker, the only sign of tension other than his unnatural stillness.

'Are you in all seriousness telling me, Sir Charles, that a bank of your standing, with all its international connections, would refuse to honour the authenticated instructions of one of its most important clients?'

'In law, the definition of the word "instructions" becomes somewhat equivocal in these circumstances. I am told that such a document would have the same status as evidence produced under torture. I mean no direct comparison, of course, but the possibility of signature under duress would, I assure you, render the instructions null.'

'In English law, perhaps. But have you considered what the International Court at The Hague would have to say about all this?'

Cromer smiled. 'I understand that the International Court can deal only with disputes between nations, that is, between governments. It has nothing to say on disputes between individuals, companies or other organizations. Those are dealt with under the laws of the countries concerned. In this instance, the possibility of signature under duress would invalidate any documents under English, Swiss or American law.'

Yufru's eyes had opened wider. His mood had changed to one of incredulous anger.

'You are claiming that the Emperor's fortune can never, in any circumstances, be returned to its rightful owners. I find that an attitude of the greatest immorality. It will be

49

seen by my superiors as a most cynical expression of capitalist imperialism.'

Cromer had touched the nerve he had been probing for. Yufru's anger was a sign that Cromer's speculations had been in some way correct. Yet the anger was assertive. It revealed neither fear nor surprise. Either he was an extremely accomplished politician or, as Cromer had guessed, he had still another card to play: the threat of exposure to a wave of hysterical anti-Western propaganda. It was time to pre-empt any such possibility, and retain Yufru's goodwill.

'I fail to make myself clear, Mr Yufru. My apologies. I did not say "in any circumstances". I can imagine circumstances in which this problem might be solved in a way favourable to both of us. Perhaps the time has come to consider them . . . Your tea?'

The tea was another small piece in Cromer's game. The ritual of hospitality offered reassurance and a distraction from confrontation.

'But,' continued Cromer, 'the exercise will demand utter honesty on both sides.'

Yufru sipped, his tension dissipating, relieved that there still seemed a way forward, yet wary of Cromer's mention of honesty.

He said: 'Please go on.'

'Very well. I want to suggest to you another . . . hypothesis. I will follow it with a suggestion that should relieve you of your difficulty. I have thought long and carefully about this. It will take a little time. I would ask you not to make any reaction until I have finished.'

Cromer stood up and began to walk slowly round the room. He did not wish to seem to be addressing Yufru directly. He became discursive, donnish.

He asked Yufru to suppose, for the sake of argument, that the Emperor was still alive, and that his mission had been to discover the circumstances in which any documents the Emperor might sign in the future would be accepted by Cromer's Bank and its associates. Yufru would, of course, attempt to disguise the fact of the Emperor's survival. He would hope that Cromer would give an assurance that documents several months old would suffice. In that case, no doubt Yufru would have produced such papers. Likewise, if Cromer had demanded a recent signature, duly signed documents would have appeared, with some plausible explanation.

'What extraordinary assumptions,' commented Yufru.

'I agree. But it is my duty to consider the possibility of such a deception, and it would be wrong of me not to devise ways to prevent such a trick succeeding. In this odd game, I believe I have now succeeded.'

Yufru waited, impassively.

'What now?' continued Cromer. 'Perhaps I should say "checkmate". But that would, I believe, be short-sighted. My assumptions may be wrong. You may have alternative strategies. And, besides, it would run counter to our own banking traditions.

'Let us try another approach, and ask: in these circumstances, would your attempted duplicity be really necessary? I think not. We are by reputation honest and discreet. We would not wish to keep from you, against natural justice, money that I concede is yours. Nor would we wish to reveal to our profession, let alone the world at large, that we have paid over to you such a sum of money. Supposing the Emperor to be still alive, it would certainly be in our interests, as well as yours, to conceal the fact.

'Now, let me move on to my conclusion. As you must have already guessed, I no longer think that this is a mere intellectual exercise. I believe the Emperor is still alive. I believe you have attempted to trick us, and failed. But I also assert our community of interest. That being so, there is I believe, a way forward.

'My suggestion is as follows: that we arrange between us the necessary documents; that duly appointed representatives of the banks meet the Emperor discreetly, in circumstances that would allow us all to see that no undue pressure was, at that time, being exerted; and that thereupon all parties freely sign the documents, transferring the Emperor's fortune, or most of it, to your government.

'Now perhaps I may have your comments?'

The banker sat down again, and looked across at Yufru, who did not yet look up. Yufru poured himself another cup of tea. No sugar, no milk. He rose, walked with his cup to the window and stared down at the twilit street, a river of moving lights, silent beyond the double glazing.

'One question, Sir Charles,' he said at last, 'what, as the Americans say, would be in it for you?'

'We have a reputation to uphold. We do not like publicity. Any public dispute, as I am sure you are aware, would be bad for us, and unless we come to some arrangement you would be in a position to accuse us publicly of duplicity. Besides, once the funds are transferred to you, your country will have to keep the money somewhere. Given our past record, I am sure you will agree that Cromer's is the bank best qualified to administer it on your government's behalf. I would like to think that we shall not be losing by the transaction.'

'I see.'

Then, suddenly decisive, Yufru swung round. Cromer sat back, apparently relaxed.

'Sir Charles, the time has come to talk frankly. I am, as you know, an unofficial envoy of my government. The Ambassador here is aware of our intent to have the Emperor's fortune returned, but has not been informed of my specific role. Officially I am there to vet visa applications. In fact I report directly to the First Vice-President, Lieutenant-Colonel Mengistu Haile Mariam, by whom I am empowered to use whatever methods I can to acquire the Emperor's fortune.

'You tell me that you yourself, or your representatives, must see the Emperor sign in order to accept his signature. Very well, I confirm your guess. The Emperor is still alive. He is, of course, under house arrest, and he is no longer in Addis. If he were, rumours of his survival would be sure to leak out. He is in his birthplace, Harar, in the mountains 200 miles to the east of Addis, with a few chosen family members, in utter isolation. The palace is his own, a citadel, but it is a prison now rather than a home. There is no contact between the guards and the family. Food, drink, laundry, all is left, as it were, on the doorstep.

'The only one to go to and fro is the President's doctor. He has confirmed that the Emperor is still in remarkable health for his years. He has recovered well from his prostate operation. How long will he remain fit? We do not know. He has nothing to live for. But, as you realize, we have much to keep him alive for. There is a certain urgency. But he has so far refused to discuss the transfer of his money, fortunately for both of us as it turns out.

'You say it is in your interests to effect a discreet solution to this problem. It is certainly in ours. Sir Charles, your proposal is . . . very helpful. I must take further advice. Perhaps we could meet, say, tomorrow morning?'

* * *

Rourke meanwhile had written himself a nice little sub-plot. He could do with a bit of R and R, but he also knew that there would be no chance of freelance earnings like this once he was back with the Regiment. Whatever Collins was offering, he wanted. So he would call, as planned, and he would go, if asked. That left him with one night for Lucy. He had planned to call her from his parents, when he had been re-civilized by baths, aftershave and good cooking, but these were exceptional times.

'Luce?'

Good that she had answered. She didn't like him calling the shop, because it meant grief from the Patels, who owned the place.

'Michael bloody Rourke. Where are you, you bad boy?'

'Airport. You free tonight?'

'What do you think? I keep myself free just on the off chance? No, I ain't.'

He heard the banter in her tone, and played along.

'Look, Luce, it's an emergency. I think I'll be out of here again tomorrow. I came all this way just to see you.'

'Oh, sure. Look, I can't talk now. There's people here.'

'What time?'

'I told you: I can't.'

Oh, shit. She sounded serious.

'Why not?'

'Listen. I get off at six. Meet me then. I'll explain. Got to go.'

'It's almost six now! I'll never – Luce? Shit!'

She had hung up. Meet her where? The shop? Her place – wherever that was?

He took a bus into town, rode east on the tube, and walked down the road, past the laundrette and the Moti Mahal and the arcade games, to the shop. It was closed. He banged on the door without any real hope, and slung his pack down with a sigh of disgust.

The curtains behind the wire mesh parted. Lucy looked out at him briefly. He couldn't read her expression. He saw nothing of her but a mass of black curls and a pair of dark eyes. 'What kept you?' came her muffled voice.

'I . . .'

'Never mind,' she said, as she came out and slammed the door behind her. She was angry.

'What's up?' he asked.

'You think you can swan in any time from anywhere, blow in my ear, and I'll follow you anywhere.'

'I wrote,' he said, slinging his pack on his shoulder. 'Come on, Luce, I'll buy you a drink.'

'Look, there's something I have to explain.'

He stared at her. This was not good.

She glanced round. 'But not here.'

'I thought we could go to the hotel.'

'You really are a bastard,' she said, expressionless. 'You know that?'

'It's all your fault.'

She smiled, sadly, and said with a hint of irony: 'It's nice of you to say so.'

'I mean it. You made me want you.'

'I know what you mean, you daft bugger. You don't have to explain.' She looked at him. 'Go to the hotel. I'll find you there.'

'What are you going to do?'

'Never you mind.'

'OK. Don't be long. I'll get something in for supper.'

She left the alley and walked quickly down the street without turning back.

He picked up his pack, and walked fast in the opposite direction. It was a mile to the Floral Court, where they had first made love before he went to Rhodesia. It had few rivals in this part of east London, because there was not much call for a hotel. Its main source of income was the bar, all bare boards and Victorian mirrors, which supported a hard-drinking darts team and several bar-billiards fanatics. The rooms were merely a way for Pat Sargeant to cash in on the building she had inherited from her father. Now in her fifties, she had never married, and was thus one of those rare creatures, an independent woman. She was short, sturdy, immensely hard-working and she made people laugh. The reason she worked so hard and kept so fit and remained happy, in the midst of fumes and garbage and graffiti, was that she could escape whenever she wanted to a cottage near Maidstone, on a farm where she had been a hop-picker as a kid. Some weekends, and for two weeks in the summer, she would vanish, closing the place up. In autumn, she would drape the bar in hop-bines to remind her of the country and her childhood. Originally the place had been called the George. It was she who had renamed it Floral Court.

When Rourke entered, Pat was behind the bar, a fizz of grey hair and huge glasses, serving a pint to one of the half-dozen customers. She glanced up, smiled a welcome, then frowned, remembering. He stood waiting, until she came across to him. She stared quizzically, saying nothing.

'No,' she said, at last. 'Brain's going. It's that disease that makes you forget. Put me out of my misery.'

'Rourke.'

'Yes. Michael. Got you. You were off to Australia.'

'Africa.'

'Well, same sort of area. And you had a pretty girl.'

'Lucy.'

'That's the one. Dark hair, nice bum. Still around, is she?'

'Pat, I need the room again. Is it free?'

'It could be. It depends.'

'On?'

'On whether you intend to use it for its designated purpose.'

'Which is?' he asked, smiling.

'You tell me. You get the right answer, you get the room.'

'Oh, come on. She'll be here in a minute. I need a bath.'

'Ah, now we get to it. Young man . . .' She wagged a finger at him, frowning. 'I know your sort. You want to sully my nice clean room with filthy behaviour, you want to indulge your gross carnal habits in an orgy of unmitigated lust.'

'Well, yes.'

'With Lucy?'

He nodded.

She cracked a smile, and flicked a glass, making it ring. 'Ding! That is the right answer. Twenty-five a night, and you make your own coffee. Get on up. Remember the way?'

The room was as it had been. One of those high, old-fashioned double beds with slatted wooden ends, a Victorian grate of intricately stamped metal, bedside tables with ornate doilies, two ancient bulbous armchairs and a low round table, wardrobe, sink, mirror, kettle, coffee jar. It seemed as if no one had been in the room since he and Lucy were there five months previously.

He slung his pack in the wardrobe, pulled out a fresh if crumpled T-shirt, ran himself a bath in the bathroom next door, shaved, made a coffee, and lay on the bed. All the while, his mind was racing ahead. Lucy was different. She had always been sharp, but never like this: angry, distracted, secretive. He could think of reasons, and didn't like to take any of them seriously. All he wanted was her. No point in forcing a row.

He was beginning to wonder whether she was really coming, whether she had sent him ahead just to get rid of him – and what then? Would he go to her house? Was she still living at home? – when he heard footsteps on the stairs.

She came in, and watched deadpan as he stood up and came to her. She had changed out of her working jeans into a skirt. She was still wearing the same sweater. He took her hand.

'Luce? What's the matter, beauty?'

'Don't "beauty" me. You can't . . .' She stopped short, and he heard a catch in her voice. 'Look.' Her voice was softer, almost pleading. 'I can't.'

He stood looking at her blankly. 'What?'

She hardened again, and when she spoke her voice rose in anger. 'You were away so long. I didn't know where you were, when you were coming back. You bastard. You *bastard*.' She hit him on the chest. He caught her hand as it came down a second time.

'Hey,' he said gently, holding her. 'Come on now.'

And whether she fell into his arms or whether he took her neither could tell, but suddenly she was there, and his face was in her neck, and she was crying against him. 'Hey,' he said again, and kissed her neck, then her ear, her hair, her damp cheek, and finally her mouth. They kissed as they had kissed the night before they parted, five months before, deep and full. His hand was under her sweater, sliding from the waist of her jeans on to her bare back. No bra, as ever. His hand went right up her back to the nape of her neck, holding her head against his shoulder.

'Oh, Mike,' she said. 'Oh, Mike.'

The urgency of her response and the switchback changes of signal – the rejection, the anger, the tension, the desire – told him all he needed to know.

He said, still holding her: 'There's another bloke.'

'Yes.'

He knew her well enough to understand everything all at once. She wasn't in love with this other guy, because if she had been she would never have agreed to see him. But she was in deep enough to be frightened, deep enough to be concerned that she shouldn't be seen with Rourke. He was only back for a day or two, then he'd be gone, for God knew how long, and she had a life to live, and what was she supposed to do?

None of this she needed to say. What mattered to him most was that she still wanted him. Because he wanted her, right now, so much that this other bloke really didn't exist. He belonged to yesterday and tomorrow. Today it was the two of them, and nothing else.

She pulled back. 'I can't stay,' she said.

'Lucy, don't do this to me. I love you.'

'You said that before. Then you went away, and you'll go away again, and I have to stay here and look after Mum and work and . . .'

'Don't talk. Get undressed.'

'No! Mike! I'm meant to be out for a walk. Out for a walk!' she repeated bitterly. 'I never go out for walks. I'll have some explaining to do.'

She didn't want to tell him all the truth – his name, what he did, why she was so frightened of him – because she knew he didn't want to know, and he knew she knew.

He drew her to him again, and felt her melt into him, felt the pressure of her stomach, groin and thighs. Again his hand slipped up her back. She shuddered as they kissed.

He locked his arm behind her back, and lifted her towards the bed, still kissing her. She made one last attempt to restrain herself, and him, by not lying back. Instead, she sat. But her legs were apart, and to keep on the same level as her, he knelt.

It was merely a ritual delay. They both knew that now.

'Mike, I have to be careful.'

'I know, my darling.'

'I don't want anyone to know I'm here.'

'They won't.'

Bastard. Liar. His senses were full of her, and right then he would have said anything to get her into bed.

And she wanted to believe. As his hand went beneath her skirt, feeling for the top of her knickers – she was wearing the underwear he had always admired, the silk ones with pretty decorative edges – she raised herself so that he could slip them off.

There was a tradition to their lovemaking, well enough established to thrill them both with the knowledge of what was coming next. First, she had to come, somehow, it didn't matter how, against his thigh, against his stomach – she was so wrapped in the power of her desire she didn't care how. This time, he gave her his mouth, kneeling, while she leant back, her back thrusting up from the edge of the bed. He drew her deep into him, working with lips and tongue until he felt her quiver and relax.

Only then did he rise, lift her languid body into bed, slide off her sweater, and at last undress himself.

This next chapter in their lovemaking was also not extended. She was too ready to come again, and he was far too aroused for delay. It didn't matter, because they both knew – whatever she had said earlier – that there would be at least one, perhaps two later opportunities that night.

At some point, while recovering, her hair strewn across his chest and her thigh tight around his waist, he dozed off.

'Hey,' she said digging him in the ribs. 'You said you were going to get supper.'

'I forgot,' he said.

'Bastard,' she said, with a smile. 'I'm hungry.'

'Well, eat,' he said.

Her smile broadened. 'OK. Here I come,' and he felt her lips work their way down his hard, flat stomach.

4

Not far away late that night, while Rourke and Lucy lay cupped like spoons asleep, Peter Halloran and Frank Ridger were walking down an alley near Ridger's rented house. Halloran had bought Ridger a drink. A few days ago, this would have been surprising. But Halloran had taken to going out now and then, and not merely to counteract the boredom. Like a predator, he wanted to know his territory. It was during such a prowl that he had phoned Collins and received the tip-off. Never one to take a chance, he had at once assumed the worst, and had acted accordingly. Ridger had been happy to pull on his old overcoat and go along with his volatile, talkative house guest.

'Come along this way,' said Halloran, looking down a darkened alley, 'we've not been down here.'

'There ain't nothing down there.'

'Further along there is,' replied Halloran. 'A club. I was out walking earlier and noticed it. Perhaps we'll get a last drink.'

At the end of the street there was a call-box, the one Halloran had used to contact Collins. A few yards away was an abandoned building site, surrounded by a wire-mesh fence, leaning, battered and in places flattened by local kids. It was a mournful place. A year ago the square had been a block of decaying slum houses. In two years' time, no doubt, there would be council flats that would soon be equally tawdry. But at the moment the place looked like a bomb-site. The few street-lights cast long shadows behind the piles of rubble, disguising pits and puddles.

Halfway down the alley, Halloran said: 'Well, Frank, you have been the soul of hospitality. But I'm afraid it's time to be moving along.'

With only the briefest of pauses, Ridger said: 'Oh? Why's that, then?'

'Itchy feet. I get the strange feeling I'm being watched.'

'That's silly, that is. Why, no one knows you're here.'

'I get the funny impression they do. I can tell, you see. Eyes in the back of my head. Comes from years of action. Take today: I just got an overwhelming sense of people closing in. Eyes' – his arm swung expressively – 'everywhere. How do you explain that?' And his right arm came up to rest on the older man's shoulder.

'Well . . . I can't explain why you should feel that way, can I? Anyway you've no need to worry. You're safe here.'

'Now, Frank, don't tell me you'd not rather I was gone. Not much social life with me here, is there? You have friends. You've been calling a few. I know, you see.'

Ridger's shoulders tensed under Halloran's hand.

'Holy Mother, how do you . . .? You've been watching me . . . Well, what does it matter? I can have friends, can't I?'

'Of course you can. But it makes me nervous. Now, who was it you were calling on your way home today?'

'Just a pal. We arranged . . . a drink for Saturday.'

'Oh, yes. I'd like to meet him, too. I'm getting lonely as hell, you know. What's his name?'

'Come on, Peter, what do you need his name for?'

'And number. Let's arrange a threesome.' They were nearing the end of the darkened street, ten yards short of the phone box, its single light-bulb casting a pale glow on the damp pavement. 'We'll call him from here.'

'Oh, no, Peter. We can't do that.'

Ridger's prevarication turned Halloran's suspicions into blinding certainty.

'I think I know why not.' And with that, Halloran's left arm came round and slammed the air out of Ridger's lungs. The older man doubled up. Halloran hauled him vertical against the wall, grabbed a handful of hair, forced his head back and stared into his face. Ridger, open-mouthed, dumb, struggled to fill the collapsed tissue under his ribs.

'You see, I have reason to believe your friend was no friend of mine. How much do you get paid for shopping me? Hundred quid? Is that the going rate round here' – Halloran began to bang Ridger's head against the wall on each emphatic word – 'for a – wild – boy – like – me?'

Ridger began to recover his voice.

'Christ . . . oh, Christ . . . I never told . . . I swear . . . let me be.'

Halloran saw that Ridger was near to collapse. It was time for another tack, for there was more to Halloran than pure violence.

He relaxed his grip on Ridger's hair, and set both his hands on Ridger's shoulders, supporting him. His brow furrowed, as if in displeasure. He would have made a good interrogator.

'Look, I don't blame you, Frank. We all work for money. But I've got to know, see. Self-defence. If I don't know, I have to guess, and that's when people get hurt needlessly. If I know, I can plan. So tell me . . . Quiet now.'

A young man approached down the street, a labourer in denim jacket and jeans, his gait showing him to be the worse for a few pints. Halloran held Ridger's shoulder more lightly.

As the stranger disappeared round the corner, Halloran continued in a low, persuasive voice: 'They'll never know you helped me. I'll just vanish. Come on, come on now. Jesus, aren't we from the same lovely island? I'm frightened, can't you see? I don't like hitting friends.'

He relaxed his grip. Ridger was breathing more easily.

'Let's talk now, Frank. Come along over this way, where it's quiet and nobody can hear us.' And he took Ridger by the arm and began to lead him past the call-box, across the road to the darkness of the building site.

'I'll avoid the lights, if you don't mind,' he remarked, and gave an abrupt laugh. As they stepped over part of the flattened fence, Halloran produced a torch from the pocket of his anorak to guide them.

Ridger, his voice trembling with shock, but apparently reassured, said: 'All right, then. The coppers were on at me at work, me and a few others. Somebody had tipped them off about you. They know I'm a linkman. They were going to run me in. I want to be out of it. I'm too old for this business. Oh, Jesus. Peter, let me be. Let me be. I don't know what they'll do.'

They were picking their way slowly across the waste ground, the piles of rubble silhouetted against the distant street lamps.

'They won't be doing nothing to you, friend,' Halloran told him solicitously. 'I'll make sure they don't. Let's see if we can find a drink, then. Watch this hole, now.'

They came level with a shadowy pit dug to test the subsoil months earlier.

Halloran's right hand moved again across Ridger's shoulders, as if to guide him. As it did so, the left hand came up to the other shoulder. It held a three-foot length of thin rope with a small weight at the end. The rope swung before Ridger was aware. The weight smacked into Halloran's right hand as the noose snapped taut around Ridger's neck.

His death was silent. His face screamed, but no sound came. Blood and air were locked off in an instant. Halloran applied pressure by crossing his arms. It took Ridger thirty seconds to become unconscious and another two minutes to die, on his knees, forced down and then supported by Halloran's iron grip.

When it was over, Halloran rolled the body into the hole and threw bricks down on it until it was covered with rubble. He checked his work with his torch, tossed some more bricks in and checked again. There was no sign of the body.

He then replaced the rope in his pocket and headed over the rubble-strewn square towards a workmen's hut. To one side of it was a hod for gravel and stones once used in the making of a path across the mud. In the hod he had left his few belongings – his rucksack, containing a few rough clothes. He couldn't risk going back to Ridger's house.

But as if to prove himself right, he approached it and waited in the shadows a hundred yards away. Near the house was a parked car, side-lights on, with two men in it. After ten minutes, as a few late-night drinkers ambled past and the house remained dark, Halloran saw, by the light of the street lamp, the driver's hand come up towards his face. Halloran, recognizing the action of a man speaking into a microphone, knew the men to be police.

He nodded grimly, muttered: 'Wait on, you bastards,' and headed away.

He walked for twenty minutes, hopped on a bus and went into Leytonstone tube station, to cross town for the anonymity of Earls Court.

As far as the waiting Special Branch men were concerned, both Irishmen had vanished completely. A search of Ridger's house was later to reveal fingerprints, but no further clues. Ridger's body was found only two months later, when work started again on the site.

Halloran broke his journey at Paddington and went into a call-box to contact Collins. It was approaching midnight.

'Pity you're late, Peter,' said Collins, 'but not to worry. We're on, at least so far. Where are you now?'

'Paddington, Major, but I won't be here overnight. I took your warning. I reckon it saved me a turn inside. But I have to drop out of sight soon, for a long, long time.'

'That'll suit us all. There's a train around midday. If you catch it, you should see Michael Rourke. He's our number three. A good team, don't you think?'

Wednesday, 24 March
Yufru arrived at Cromer's office at 10.30 a.m.

'Sir Charles,' he said as he sipped a coffee, 'I had a most interesting evening. Mengistu is in agreement that the money must be released at all costs. There must be no risks, no delays. We are to work together to draw up suitable documents and make arrangements for their signature by the Emperor, yourselves and the Ethiopian government.'

'Congratulations, Mr Yufru. It's good to know we are moving in the same direction. Now, to come straight to the point, I have noted a number of matters that should be included in any memorandum of agreement between us. I suggest that we discuss them and that I then draft a first version of the memorandum which will be circulated to my colleagues, to your government and to the Emperor. When I have the comments on that draft, I hope we shall be able to draw up a final version acceptable to us all.

'I warn you, it will be a bulky document. But most of the space will be taken up with specifications of the Emperor's accounts and investments. In addition to these, he owns a number of companies in Europe, America and Africa. These will be the subject of a separate schedule, because they will have to be sold off if the investments are to be realized in full. Such things take time – as much as a year, I'm afraid. But the bulk of the funds is in currencies of various denominations, in gold and in Maria Theresa dollars. It should be possible to place, say, seventy-five per cent of the amounts involved to your account within a week of signature and a further ten per cent within a month.'

Yufru was taking notes in silence. Cromer reached the heart of the matter: the circumstances in which the signature would have to take place. The meeting would have to be on neutral territory. Was there any possibility of flying the Emperor to Switzerland? Mr Yufru looked up, smiled and spread his hands.

'My dear Sir Charles,' he said condescendingly, 'would you, in our position, take such a risk?'

Cromer raised his hands, as if to say: point taken.

'We were thinking,' Yufru continued, 'that we could fly you to Harar. A fascinating medieval fortress, but we also have facilities for tourism there. And, of course, the Emperor would not have to be moved.'

It was Cromer's turn to smile. 'Now, Mr Yufru, you must understand that we cannot possibly meet the Emperor in his place of imprisonment. I am sure that in such circumstances we too might feel . . . under pressure.'

The bargaining continued for an hour. Cromer suggested a number of African countries: Nigeria, Egypt, Zaïre. Yufru mentioned places in Ethiopia with the necessary tight security. Eventually Cromer said: 'Mr Yufru, there is one place that can satisfy both our criteria: an embassy in Addis Ababa, if possible the Swiss. It is the custom, is it not, for such places to be contained within their own compounds? You could provide all the security needed up to the moment the Emperor arrives. Thereafter he is on foreign soil. Your guards will be excluded. In the embassy of a neutral country we can see that no pressure is exerted. I feel that would be entirely acceptable to us.'

'Except that once again the Emperor is outside our control,' countered Yufru. 'It is possible to seek asylum in a foreign embassy.' He recalled the case of the Hungarian, Cardinal Mindszenty, who sought refuge in the American Embassy in Budapest after the Hungarian uprising in 1956. He remained there safely for fifteen years.

'Yes, I see,' said Cromer. 'You will want some assurances from the embassy concerned that they will allow appropriate measures to be taken. What have you in mind?'

'For such details I will again have to consult Addis Ababa.'

'Very well. But there is another problem that you hinted at earlier. How would the Emperor arrive?'

'I mentioned the problem of delivery within Ethiopia to the President last night. It is a relatively simple matter wherever the meeting takes place. There is only one way for top officials to travel efficiently in Ethiopia – by air. In this case, the distance is not particularly great. The Emperor would not, of course, be brought in by plane. The final stage from the airport to the embassy would require police escorts, a darkened car, the clearing of streets – all unacceptable and unnecessary. No, he would be brought in by helicopter.'

It was now 12.45. Both men needed a break. Cromer suggested that each should spend the weekend preparing a detailed proposal of the personnel to be involved and the scheduling. It would have to be in the form of a first exchange of ideas, for he feared nothing could be finalized until well into the following week. Only then could they begin the business of drafting a working agreement.

At that moment, Halloran and Rourke were approaching Oxford. The train was only a few minutes behind schedule. Collins, briefed to meet the 1.15 to Banbury, wouldn't have to wait long.

The two men had met at the ticket barrier at Paddington. Each knew the other was involved. There was a quiet satisfaction that they were on the move together again.

Rourke said: 'Peter, you mick. What have we let ourselves in for?'

'I'm no mind-reader, Michael. The major's not told me a thing. But I'll buy you a drink while we talk about it.'

They sipped Holsten lagers in the buffet car and tried to guess. Must be a small do . . . didn't say anything about weapons . . . Ireland? South America? Middle East? Don't fancy tangling with the Israelis . . . and anywhere in that part you have identity problems . . . Cyprus? West Africa? Surely not back to Rhodesia . . . wait a minute: Uganda. You think someone is trying to get at Big Daddy Amin? Now that would be something. But where's the money in that? Who'd be paying the bills?'

Despite their experience, they were no nearer a solution when Collins picked them up at Banbury station in his Range Rover.

'Good to see you again,' he said. 'Hop in and we'll have a jolly weekend huntin', shootin' and fishin'. You can pretend to be country squires for a couple of days. How does that suit you?'

The three of them had a light lunch, during which Collins explained as much as he could. It would be an undercover show, probably without weapons, in a foreign country, to kidnap a senior political element. There would be few if any guards. Neutral territory – in an embassy. There wouldn't be any problems about the job itself.

'The problem,' Collins concluded over coffee, 'will be to escape.'

Having whetted their appetite for the adventure, Collins was as good as his word. He offered them a choice of double-barrel twelve-bore Browning D5s, lent them some welling-tons, and led them out into the field behind the farm to introduce them to clay-pigeon shooting. It was a perfect day for it. The air was sparkling clear and the woods that fringed the field were tinged with the green of budding leaves.

Collins was proud of his layout. The trap, which looked like a solid box from the firing mark, actually contained an auto-matic release mechanism that fired the saucer-shaped clay discs, or 'birds', at the sound of a human voice. It was programmed not to respond to the report of a gun. Collins had demonstrated twice, and the other two had also tried their hands.

'I shout "Pull!" because that's what one shouts in a normally operated trap,' explained Collins, 'but any shout would do. Now, watch again . . . Pull!'

A disc zinged out in front of him. His gun came up smoothly, he fired and the disc shattered into a black smudge. He lowered his gun and ejected the spent cartridge.

'OK, Michael. Now remember: swing, don't aim. And shoot in front of the bird. It's moving at thirty miles an hour. OK. Stance. Lean forward . . .'

'Fuck!' shouted Rourke. A disc flew out. Rourke lifted the gun, fired and missed.

'Lost,' said Collins with a grin. 'Serves you right.'

'I was right there,' Rourke replied. 'I'll try again in a moment. Now, Major, you have to tell us more. It's totally unfair. All this is fun, but it doesn't help us.'

'I've told you all I can. You'll know more when we get the go-ahead.'

Thursday, 25 March

Cromer rose early, as usual. His life was one of very few indulgences, and even fewer human contacts. His marriage, never one of passion, had sunk back to one of mere convenience: a house, well run, a place to entertain necessary guests and an occasional shoot. His real world was the City. He wanted it to be that way, for he had for years harboured an ambition that could be satisfied only through the City, an ambition to exercise unfettered power and feel the zing of individual achievement.

He was not happy with his professional status. The gratitude towards Rothschild's that had been second nature to his grandfather and father had ebbed away. He saw only the framework that constrained him, the galling need to explain and justify his actions in monthly partners' meetings. His father had appreciated that it was just such controls that kept Cromer's stable. But Sir Charles didn't like it. He wanted independence, his own bank, the freedom his grandfather had once had. If he made a break, as he intended to someday, he would need to keep his present customers and win others. To do so, he would need to prove an unswerving, even ruthless, dedication to his clients' funds.

Here, perhaps, was the opportunity he needed.

To lose Selassie's fortune would not only be costly for the bank and a blow to his colleagues; it would show him to be a political turncoat. Who in Africa or the Middle East would trust him with future profits – from oil, perhaps, or metals – if the mere hint of political difficulty was seen to be enough to separate a rich client from his deposits? But if he was known to have preserved those deposits in the face of intense pressure – that would provide him with a name worth having!

Ambition was one motive. Another, equally powerful at this moment, was the sheer thrill of the thing. There had been too little excitement over the last twenty years. He had few interests outside business. He had no mistress. Indeed, he'd never had one. Years ago, when he had first bought the house, there had been the occasional sexual skirmish, but now desire itself had become a rarity. It was not women he loved, but gold, about which he knew a great deal, and about which he would talk with passion.

He was in good company, for the love of gold has gripped all civilizations. Its lure seems illogical: how odd, after all, to dig metal from a hole in the earth, to bury it again in another hole beneath a bank. Yet, because of its rarity, it remains the epitome of wealth, the symbol of perfection, the ultimate medium of exchange between nations, the individual's final bastion against ruin.

Indeed so hard won is gold, so expensive in cash and human life, that in all history a mere 100,000 tons have been mined, eighty per cent of that amount this century. Yet gold is so dense that all the world's supply, the bars of the world's banks and the bullion merchants, the plates and bowls of the ancient Scythians, the Aztec decorations that Cortés plundered, the world's gold coins – the doubloons, dinars, rials, mohurs, dollars, sertums, reis, levas, francs, pesos, ducats, pesetas, guilders, all of the 776 types of gold coin known to dealers – the wedding rings hoarded by Vietnamese peasants, the chocolate-sized tola bars smuggled from Dubai into India, the medals hung around the necks of Arabian women, the whole lot would, if melted together, form a cube the size of a large house, sixty feet per side.

It was part of all this – the wealth, the power, the traditions, the sheer magic of the metal – that was now at stake. Cromer, in his brown silk dressing-gown and leather slippers, brewed coffee and browsed through *The Times*. He shaved and dressed in his habitual suit, and at a few minutes past eight he sat down at his desk to list his objectives.

He needed the financial aspects to be as open as possible, for copies of everything would have to go to Yufru and thence to Addis – a vital link in the chain of confidence with which he needed to surround the scheme. He would have to call Kupferbach at home in Zurich and at the same time ask him about the possible use of the Swiss Embassy. That he could do immediately. This afternoon, Lodge in Greenwich, Connecticut. He needed to confirm to them that everything was moving and warn them about the coming telex requesting an authorized assessment of the Emperor's holdings. The computerized details would have to be retrieved, printed, copied, formally set out, signed and couriered over.

Then there was Collins, and the other two. He needed to approve their accommodation in London, provide their covers, give them information and cash, go over their ideas.

He was preparing to leave when the phone rang. It was Collins.

At a hotel near Portland Place, in a suite on the fourth floor, looking out on the Langham Hotel, that rambling, still bomb-scarred colony of the BBC, Cromer pushed a bottle of whisky towards Rourke and Halloran, on the sofa opposite. Both men were wearing dark roll-neck sweaters, under their jackets, as if they were in uniform. Cromer sat in an armchair. To his left, in a second armchair, sat Collins in tweed trousers and a corduroy jacket. Coats lay on the bed.

'Please, gentlemen, help yourselves,' Cromer said, 'my apologies for offering such anonymous hospitality.' He took in the hotel room with a sweep of his arm. 'We shall be working closely together soon enough, I hope, if all goes well. Until we're certain of that, I prefer to separate my own personal and professional life from this business as much as possible. I'm sure you understand. Now, since it is essential you waste no time in beginning your plans, let me give you the details I have so far. My name is Charles Cromer and I'm an old friend of Dicky . . .'

He spoke for over half an hour, outlining what had happened and what he needed done. He didn't specify the sums involved, but he described Yufru's role, the banking arrangements, his own central position, the fact of Selassie's survival, the need for his removal, the need to prevent the Emperor signing anything, his own plan to gain access to Selassie, the Emperor's arrival by helicopter under tight security, the apparent acceptance of the suggestions so far.

'Gentlemen,' he finished, 'there are countless details still to clarify, but I have to suggest certain conditions to the Ethiopians. To do so, I must know your requirements as soon as possible.'

Halloran poured himself a slug of whisky, and glanced at Rourke. Collins spoke first.

'Don't expect answers right away, Charlie. It's a tricky operation. Not the normal run of things at all. We're used to . . .'

'Stop, Dicky, stop,' broke in Cromer, raising his hands. 'Let's first look at the problem in general terms. What I want to know is, whether we should be proceeding at all. Is it, in theory, possible?'

He was certain Collins would say yes. But the other two had just learned the true scope of the proposal.

Halloran spoke. 'First things first. Getting in, now. I'd like a little reassurance that it wouldn't be all up to us.'

'I hope that won't be too hard. The problem should really be mine,' Cromer answered. 'To the Ethiopians, you are my advisers. You will not be required to say anything much, but must be prepared to look and act the part of bankers. No problem for you, Dicky. As for you other two, neither of you looks too extreme. I thought of crediting you to my Swiss and American counterparts, but there is a chance you'll meet Yufru, so you'll have to be juniors of my own bank. As for your actual arrival, you'll be part of an official delegation. I have no idea how you'll be treated. They may want to hush up your presence. Or you may be passed off as another visiting delegation. Or you may get an official reception. From your point of view, it won't matter. The point is, they will believe you to be bankers and will treat you accordingly, with every courtesy.'

'Passports?' asked Halloran.

'You should have fake identities.'

'You can fix it?'

'No. That's part of your job. I'll do whatever is necessary: money, documentation. Any insoluble problems?'

Collins answered this time: 'We've not done it before but we can find out.'

Again Rourke and Halloran glanced at each other. They both nodded.

Cromer pressed home his advantage. 'It's getting out that'll be the problem. You'll be in hostile country, with an old man on your hands. So let me give you some figures that I hope will make it all worthwhile. My offer is this: £100,000 for each of you.'

Halloran rounded his lips.

'In three stages,' Cromer continued. 'Ten thousand as an advance, payable now. That is, of course, inclusive of the £1000 I guaranteed for you to make yourselves available in the first place. A further £20,000 upon the successful completion of the planning. And the balance upon your return. I would naturally be willing to arrange payment in any currency in the country of your choice. I should remind you that we have excellent contacts in Switzerland.'

After Cromer had gone, Collins placed an order for a supper of fillet steak all round. Then, while he was in the bathroom, Rourke and Halloran agreed the money was good, and that there was a fair chance of success.

Collins made way for Halloran to relieve himself and poured himself a whisky. When Halloran returned, Collins said: 'Let's start at the beginning. I think we can act our part as bankers.'

'Any micks in the City?' asked Rourke with a smile.

'Or fucking barrow-boys?' countered Halloran

'Not all City people are public school,' said Collins. 'Besides, you won't have to speak much, and I hardly think the Ethiopians will be fussy about accents. You will have to acquire a certain deference to me, which will be hard for you two. Your job, I imagine, will be to handle the documents, of which there are likely to be a fair number. Any problems there?'

Halloran said: 'I want to get something straight. Where are we going to work? I don't much like the idea of being in London.'

'Indeed,' said Collins, 'we all have an interest in keeping you hidden.'

Rourke agreed. 'We're going to need equipment, phones, plans, maps. We need your house. We can't work out of a hotel.'

'OK. Let's move on, then. Assume we can get there. How do we actually do the job? It has to be done rapidly and silently. There will be others – officials, government people both with Selassie and outside, but probably not many. For one thing, they won't want to attract attention to the operation by having a mass of people. For another, we can make it one of our conditions – a matching delegation, perhaps. After all, the whole point of the op is to see that no undue pressure is being placed on the old man. So let's say three of us, three of them, and Selassie, all together in one room. Where do we go from there?'

Halloran leapt in: 'We have silenced pistols. We take them out. Simple.'

Rourke grinned. 'Peter, you bloody mick!'

Halloran shrugged. 'OK, it's impossible. Just tell me why, clever Dick, and I'll forget it.'

'You think we would risk carrying hardware with us? What if they search us at the airport? Might be routine. Fine lot of bankers we'd look then, eh? Blimey, no wonder they wanted you out of Ireland. You'd sink the bloody place all by yourself, you would.'

Halloran took the rebuke in good humour. 'All right, all right. Knives then,' he said.

They each pondered the implications.

'Messy,' said Collins, 'and not so quick in a group. You have to get to each one individually. Anything could go wrong. And we might not even reach Selassie before someone got out of the room.'

'Right,' said Rourke, 'and they're not all that quiet. I remember once in Rhodesia, one of our guys had to take out a guard. He was dead in ten seconds but the noises – grunts, groans, enough to wake the dead, let alone the living! Guards outside, embassy staff, we don't want them joining the party. Anyone screams, that's it.'

He paused, then said: 'What I reckon is, we need another room. Separate them out and then a bit of close-quarter combat.'

'Ah, now you're talking,' Halloran broke in quickly. 'The old silencer.' And from beneath his sweater round his neck he pulled the rope with which he had strangled Ridger. 'No noise at all. A little slow, but effective.'

Collins grimaced: 'That's what you used the other night?'

'It is.'

Collins turned to Rourke: 'Michael, have you ever . . .?'

'No. But I've done enough karate to see us through this job.'

'All right, then,' said Collins, 'I keep in training too. It sounds a possibility.'

The other two nodded.

'Not bad odds,' said Rourke, 'if we get it set up right.'

Collins poured himself another whisky and fetched some ice from the fridge. The other two remained silent as he continued: 'Let's get to the real problem: the escape. If it doesn't seem feasible in theory we have to stop right here. I've been thinking of some possibilities. Fortunately, someone else has done a similar job just recently. I looked out some of my cuttings. It may be helpful to review it . . .'

'Carlos,' broke in Rourke. Collins smiled. Halloran looked blank.

'Peter, you should read more,' said Collins. 'You might learn something. That raid on the OPEC HQ in Vienna three months ago, remember? It offers a few parallels with our own little job . . .'

And for ten minutes he summarized the operation.

Four days before Christmas 1975, eleven ministers of the world's oil-rich nations and over fifty staff were in conference at the headquarters of the Organization of Petroleum Exporting Countries, a white-fronted building on Vienna's Ringstrasse, the tree-lined boulevard that circles the inner city. Carlos, the *nom de guerre* of a twenty-six-year-old Venezuelan terrorist named Ilich Ramírez Sánchez, and five others entered the building, killed three men, stormed the conference room on the third floor, and held all those present at gunpoint. Meanwhile, a British Special Branch officer had phoned a warning to the city's police HQ. Eight Austrian riot squad commandos arrived soon afterwards, to be driven off by bursts of fire from the watching terrorists.

Carlos was in full control. That afternoon and throughout the night he issued his demands: the broadcast of a rambling statement in support of world revolution, the provision of a bus to take them to the airport, and a DC8 to fly them to any destination he named. The plan – as Sheikh Yamani, Saudi Arabia's Oil Minister and a prime target, later revealed – was to take hostages, depart and then shoot Yamani and the Iranian Oil Minister, Dr Jamshid Amouzegar, the representatives of the two most right-wing of the OPEC countries.

The Austrian Chancellor, Bruno Kreisky, gave Carlos precisely what he wanted. The plane left as planned for Algiers to release all the hostages except Yamani and Amouzegar, and then flew on to Tripoli, Libya. At this point the operation ran out of steam because Carlos failed to receive delivery of the longer-range Boeing 707 that he needed to get him to his final sanctuary, Baghdad. Instead, he ordered the DC9 to return to Algiers, where he eventually surrendered the two remaining hostages. In return – and presumably as a reward for successfully disrupting the work of the OPEC capitalists – he received a million pounds, supplied almost certainly by the eccentric Libyan leader Colonel Gaddafi, patron of world revolution. Carlos and his fellow-terrorists were allowed to go free by the Algerians.

'There are several things of importance for us in this affair,' concluded Collins. 'The main point is that the team got in and out successfully. How? By knowing intimately in advance the ground plan of the building. By knowing the strength of the opposition. And by having hostages of such value that their demands were met instantly. As a result, they were then in a position to kill their two prime hostages with impunity, although as it happened Carlos decided not to.'

'Hostages,' pondered Halloran.

'Wouldn't work,' said Rourke, after only the briefest of pauses. 'Selassie wouldn't count. He's only worth something to the Ethiopians if he's in their hands. If we're going to take him away, they'll be better off with us all dead. None of the others would matter that much, either. We wouldn't even get out of the embassy.'

Collins nodded. 'Agreed. That's a non-starter, then. So how do we get out?'

Again it was Rourke who spoke. 'The helicopter. If that's really part of their arrangements.'

'A real genius you are!' said Halloran, wrapping an arm around Rourke's shoulder.

'You can fly?' asked Collins, looking at Rourke.

'Course. I went through the Army Air Corps for the Green Jackets in the early '60s, before the SAS.'

'Good. That makes two of us. I did a civilian course not too many years back. How about you, Peter?'

'Not one of my many talents. But with you two aces, I shan't worry.'

'It's not quite that easy,' Collins pointed out. 'We have to know the type of machine, and then make sure we can fly it.'

Gradually, as the theory of the operation became clearer, other practical questions began to emerge. Collins again pointed out the lessons of Carlos's success. They would need detailed information on the building, the personnel, the timing, the positioning of guards, the type of helicopter, the flight path after take-off. And they would need additional help – a helicopter would not have a range of more than 300 miles. They would either have to refuel or arrange reliable alternative transport. Failure on that point had curtailed Carlos's plan.

At the end of another hour all three had agreed that the scheme sounded possible in theory. That was all they needed to know. The money was good, but that was not the deciding factor. The real lure was the thrill of the thing.

When Cromer returned, he listened to the conclusions and nodded at Collins's last words: 'There's one thing we'll need – details of the building. If it is the Swiss Embassy, we have to know soon, and then get plans of the place.'

'I'll do what I can,' said Cromer. 'I'll be in touch tomorrow evening.'

5

Friday, 26 March

Cromer arrived at his office at 8.30. He had an hour to himself, and wished to be completely clear about what he would need to propose. One task would be a formal telex to both New York and Zurich requesting a schedule of the Emperor's holdings, with delivery by courier, at the weekend. But most important, he would have to prepare a letter to Selassie, persuading him to sign the transfer. He looked at the notes he had scrawled the previous day. From them, he would be able to dictate a first draft to Valerie Yates.

As usual, Valerie arrived at 9.15. At twenty-nine she already had the formal, ageless look of the top personal assistant. She always wore a suit, her light hair loose, but never more than shoulder length, with a touch of lipstick that she was at pains to renew several times a day. She was, in a word, impeccable. She knew her role and played it well.

She was only mildly dismayed at her boss's presence. Sometimes, if he had been in the country, she had that time to herself, a few minutes to prepare her desk for the day. The veneer of efficiency carefully polished was part of the framework of her professional life, itself utterly apart from the other world of her private life. She had never shown a flicker of emotion to any member of the bank. She knew that suited Sir Charles. It certainly suited her.

She prepared coffee, took the tray through, and offered a cup to Cromer, who accepted it with: 'Ten minutes, Miss Yates, please,' scarcely glancing up from his notes. She received the mail from one of the two delivery boys, opened it and set it in the leather folder stamped with the bank's seal. Then she checked her own stationery and knocked again on Cromer's door. He began to speak as soon as she sat down.

'Miss Yates, I shall need your help this week as I have never needed it before. The matter, as you will see, is of extreme delicacy. If anything leaks out, even within the company, we shall all suffer. We shall need a separate cabinet for the files and the correspondence.'

'Very well, Sir Charles.'

'You will see the nature of the problem as we go along. The first letter is to Emperor Haile Selassie.' Valerie glanced up. 'No, he is not dead, Miss Yates. He is very much alive, and we are about to persuade him to sign certain documents which will make over most of his fortune to the present government. Hence Mr Yufru's visits.

'The first major hurdle is the Emperor himself. After I have dictated the letter, look out all the usual forms of address – Conquering Lion of Judah, Elect of God, King of Kings – the whole thing. He's still a client even if he doesn't rule the place.'

He waited until Valerie had settled herself and then dictated the letter he had prepared:

'Your Highness,

'It is with overwhelming joy that I have learned of Your Highness's survival throughout these last months. I understand that your circumstances are much changed, for which I offer

86

my condolences. With the respect that we have always shown Your Highness, I would like to make a proposal concerning your affairs.

'As you are no doubt aware, the Provisional Military Administrative Council claims your assets as its own. We can confirm that under the laws of the countries in which the deposits are made, no transfer is possible without your free, written consent. This you have wisely withheld.

'But I would like to bring to Your Highness's attention a further consideration. There are numerous members of your family abroad, many of whom would, in happier circumstances, inherit a certain share of your wealth. Should you die intestate, without leaving a will that we can authenticate as valid, the family, by your own orders, receives nothing.

'I do not believe this to represent your own original intentions. Considering therefore,

– that your assets may in future be blocked in perpetuity unless you take the actions necessary to release them;

– that your family would in these circumstances be destitute;

– that the present government, through whom I must act as the *de facto* power in your country, would not countenance a direct transfer of all assets to your family;

'I make the following proposition:

'That I and my colleagues draw up the necessary documents to transfer an agreed sum to your family and an agreed sum to the present government.

'These documents having been drawn up and approved by Your Highness and the present government, I will authorize a small delegation to witness the signature on neutral territory yet to be decided and in circumstances in which Your Highness would be seen to be free of all pressure.

'I beg you to consider for your family's sake, as well as your nation's, the multiplicity of benefits that would flow from such an action, one that would reflect the greatness of your lineage.

'If Your Highness agrees in principle to this suggestion, I will make detailed proposals as soon as possible.'

Cromer paused. He was pleased with his words. The implication was strong that his last imperial act would be a generous one that would redound to Selassie's credit – and thus to the discredit of Mengistu. The fact that such ringing phrases were designed to accomplish the precise opposite of their stated intentions gave Cromer a tingle of satisfaction.

He then dictated a telex to be sent to New York and Zurich, all very formal, with copies to Yufru:

'Gentlemen, in my capacity as agent for our client known as Lion and under the terms of that agency, I request you to provide me with an inventory of Lion's assets held by you. This should be in two categories: floating assets (cash balances, gold deposits, securities) and fixed assets (those companies of which Lion has whole or part ownership). Please assess all assets at their current market value, in dollars, as of today's rates. I request that such information be delivered to me by standard courier by Thursday next week, together with a summary of information as yet unavailable, if any.'

Lodge and Kupferbach would be amused by the formal pomposity of the request. But Yufru and his bosses should be impressed. He told Valerie to put the telex out at once, keeping two copies, making the tapes herself and bringing them back upstairs with her. Of course, he had no control over what happened to the print-outs at the other end, but they were unlikely to go further and no one in London would know they had been sent.

The two items had taken half an hour to dictate. It was 10.15. Yufru should arrive shortly.

'Thank you, Miss Yates. And more coffee, I think.'

Yufru arrived promptly. The two men could now dispense with the intellectual skirmishing that had characterized their previous meetings. Valerie closed the door, and Yufru sat down at once in his usual place and poured himself a coffee. Cromer sat down opposite.

'Basically, Sir Charles,' began Yufru, 'your proposals are acceptable. The Provisional Military Administrative Council agreed that a banking delegation should witness Selassie's signature in Addis Ababa on neutral territory. Your suggestion of the Swiss Embassy is a good one. The Russian compound would be ideal from our point of view, but the Russians would not take kindly to your inevitable request for the removal of all troops on the day in question. Neither the British nor the American Embassy would be acceptable to us; they are too large and we feel the problems of security would be unnecessarily magnified. As for the African countries . . . although we are still host to the OAU I am afraid that some of our African friends are neither as friendly nor as conscientious as we should like.'

Yufru went on to explain the advantages of the Swiss Embassy. It was set in its own compound, like many of the major embassies, and also stood apart from the city centre. Given the fact that Switzerland was a major depository for the Emperor's funds, it made good sense to hold the meeting there.

'Excellent,' replied Cromer. 'I should imagine my Swiss colleagues can easily establish good contacts with the embassy in Addis. Now: your conditions.'

'We have three. One is that the telephones and telexes must be cut off during the time of the Emperor's presence in the embassy. The reason for this request is obvious: the Emperor would otherwise be given his only possible opportunity to re-establish links with the outside world.

'The other two conditions demand more positive Swiss co-operation. The signing must take place on a Sunday, so that there will be no staff on the premises. And we must provide an official presence of some kind, to ensure that the Emperor's timetable is adhered to. A defection within the embassy would be a severe embarrassment. Now, Sir Charles, you will no doubt have some further points.'

'The size of the delegation, Mr Yufru. I suggest that your delegation should match my own. I shall send a senior aide and two juniors. The bureaucratic procedure alone is considerable. My senior aide will be an expert on the Emperor's liquid assets, in particular his gold holdings. One of the two juniors will be supervising our arrangements with lawyers and company matters. The second will be there simply to ensure the various documents are correctly presented and collated. It would be diplomatic to arrange for two people to sit opposite us with Selassie. That, I feel, would be a balance of forces.'

'Not quite, Sir Charles. The Emperor can hardly be said to be on our side. Three of you should be matched by three of us.'

'Very well,' said Cromer, with a magnanimous sweep of his right hand.

'And we will, of course, provide additional guards to ensure the sealing of the embassy. The compound gates will be locked, and the two-man helicopter crew should be able to take on that particular role.'

Cromer needed to probe for information as deeply as possible without arousing suspicion.

'So we shall expect one helicopter with . . . six people including the Emperor? All coming from Harar?'

'No, no, Sir Charles. The three who will accompany the Emperor will be government members and will be in Addis already. One will be the interpreter. The other two will arrive separately by car. Is it important?'

'I suppose not, except that it seems you hold all the cards. Let's look on the black side. What if the Emperor raises insuperable problems? What guarantee have we of the diplomatic immunity normally assured by an embassy? It seems to me we could have more . . .'

'Oh, come, Sir Charles, you surely don't imagine that we would kidnap you all or shoot you. My government needs the money. If there were problems, we should, of course, make communications available to you. And you are at liberty to inform your embassy of your presence in Addis, though naturally not the reason for your presence. Our only interest is in arranging for a successful conclusion to the mission, for your rapid return and for the Emperor's . . . removal.'

Cromer nodded slowly. The conditions seemed acceptable, in line with the previous night's discussion. The timing, the transport, the setting, the personnel had virtually been decided.

As Yufru was agreeing to check the details with Addis, Valerie entered with a draft of Cromer's letter to the Emperor. She handed it and a copy to Cromer, together with a copy of his telex to Zurich and New York. Cromer thanked her as she left and glanced through the letter.

'Good,' he said, 'not yet perfect, but good enough for you to have a copy, Mr Yufru. Would you read this carefully over the next few hours and call me with any changes you think necessary? Then I will prepare a formal copy for delivery, via yourself, to the Emperor.'

'It can be in his hands within a day,' said Yufru, as he stood up to go. 'We shall talk again later.'

After he had gone Cromer recalled Yufru's mention of the Emperor's 'removal'. His pause before the word spoke volumes. The Emperor was doomed. The longer he remained alive, the greater the risk of embarrassment to the military regime. Even if he survived to sign, therefore, he would be killed by the Ethiopians, to be buried no doubt in an unmarked grave without honours – exactly the death announced by the military regime nine months earlier.

After lunch, Cromer had just three more calls to make. The first was to Zurich. He spoke to Kupferbach, explaining the business about the Swiss Embassy, the Ethiopian stipulation about cutting the building off during the time of Selassie's visit, and the need for a Sunday meeting.

'We need a diplomatic link, Oswald,' concluded Cromer. 'Contact at the highest level. Do you think you can go to the top?'

'Charles, I shall arrange an appointment with both the Foreign Minister and the Finance Minister. We cannot afford to fail. Therefore I have to tell them about Selassie. That is the only thing that will open those doors and guarantee secrecy and speed.'

'That is what I thought, Oswald. But there is more. To organize this properly, we need plans of the place. We have to know exactly, to the nearest foot, about doors and hall-ways and the size of the enclosure. Tell them we have to have this information to guarantee our own security before we agree terms. Tell them that it is the only way we can prevent a massive transfer of funds out of Switzerland to the Ethiopians. Tell them anything you damn well like, but get those plans!'

Monday, 29 March
Cromer was in early. Company work was beginning to suffer. There were letters to clients, the gold committee, analysis of stock-market trends with Jeremy Squires and young Sackville-Jones – things that should not be delayed any longer if he was to keep on top. As it was, anyone who came into his office noticed the filing cabinet against the wall. He could sense the curiosity. Here lay the explanation for the Chairman's unaccustomed remoteness. The mystery should not be allowed to deepen.

When Valerie arrived, dressed strikingly well in a dark-green skirt and matching jacket over a white blouse, Cromer told her to confirm the usual two meetings – one at 11.30, the other at three o'clock – to organize the removal of the filing cabinet back to storage and to arrange lunch upstairs with Jeremy. Squires had virtually become his deputy over the past five years. The two men scarcely knew each other socially. Squires was fifteen years Cromer's junior, but he was so damn good. Uniquely, Cromer had taken to calling him by his Christian name. Now he needed him to bring things up to date. He went on to scribble some memos, mostly probing the actions and opinions of his staff. Each combined a specialist knowledge – mining, metals, chemicals, foods – with a concern for the funds of particular clients. It had proved a useful system, building a fine combination of personal interest, expertise and general ability.

Yufru called at 11.45, when Cromer was in his first meeting, and again at 12.30, just as he was finishing.

'Sir Charles, your letter is much admired,' he said. 'A most persuasive document. We would like to transmit it at once to Selassie. When can you finalize it?'

That day, Collins, Rourke and Halloran worked out the practicalities of their plan. In the morning, Rourke took the Range Rover into Oxford and bought maps from Parker's in Broad Street. He also picked up as many handbooks on arms and weapons as he could find in Blackwells, including Jane's *All The World's Aircraft.*

Collins had his business to run and was out for the morning.

To stave off boredom, Halloran took one of Collins's twelve-bores into the spring woods. He was gone for a couple of hours.

About midday, he strolled back over the fields bearing a brace of pheasant, the gun broken across his arm.

'We're all right for supper, then,' he remarked lightly to Collins, who was washing his hands at the kitchen sink.

To his surprise Collins, who had not noticed the absence of the gun, exploded.

'You silly bugger!' he said, snatching a hand towel from a hook beside the sink. 'Did anyone see you? Sam? Molly?'

'No, I don't think so . . . What's up, would you tell me that?'

'You've never shot pheasant before, have you?'

'So?'

'Well, you don't know the bloody rules. They're protected birds. You can't just go out and shoot them any time.'

'Poor little darlings,' said Halloran, sarcastic and self-righteous. 'Fuck me, Major, here we are planning to knock off an Emperor and you're worrying about a few pheasants.'

Collins took a breath.

'Look, it's the close season now. You can only shoot pheasant between 30 September and 2 February, inclusive. Everyone knows that around here. If anyone sees you with pheasant, likely as not they'll have the law round. They're breeding. It spoils next year's shoot. And you without even a game licence! They'd be all over you, Halloran, all over you. And then all over us, OK?'

Halloran licked his lips. 'Jesus.'

Collins shook his head, returned the towel to its hook, and, seeing that he had made his point, softened.

'Well, it'll probably be all right. But I don't want Molly to get a whiff of them, and that goes for bones and feathers. So we can't eat them.'

He opened a drawer by the sink and took out a plastic disposal bag.

'Here, put them in this and bury them in the woods. You'll find a spade in the lean-to. There'll be a beer waiting for you when you get back.'

That afternoon, the three men spent a couple of hours going through books and maps. The maps allowed them to look at the options for their exit. Northwards lay Eritrea, rebellious but distant, and risky. It would mean setting up fuel dumps inside Ethiopia. A non-starter. Westwards: Sudan. Horrendous deserts, political instability, even further from an easy flight home. Eastwards: desert, crossed by a railway line. Nothing there but 'camp-sites and sheepfolds'. The border that way was closer – 300 miles from Addis – but again, who the hell was going to organize fuel dumps inside Ethiopia, let alone dumps dotted across a hideous wilderness like that? There was only one serious option: south, into Kenya.

Jane's provided a mass of information, but Collins chose to phone around his military contacts to confirm it. This

95

time, the SAS connection would be of no use. Even if he'd still been with the Regiment, this was the sort of enquiry for which he would have disguised his position.

He introduced himself for the company, saying he was preparing a report on the possible market in old aircraft in Africa. Contact led to contact, as if he was a journalist, through the Foreign Office, Army and RAF. Eventually he spoke to an officer who had been seconded to Selassie in the early 1970s and who knew the makes and numbers.

The Ethiopians had some 70,000 men under arms, and were planning a People's Militia of 150,000 as a reserve. They were aiming high, and ready to pay. Though they still had ancient Canberra B2 bombers and Second World War Dakotas as transporters, their fighter squadron was led by supersonic Northrop F5s. The helicopters were of two types: fifteen American Bell UH-IHs and the almost identical Agusta AB 205s (which are the Bells made under licence in Italy), a widely used general-purpose helicopter that carries anything up to a dozen passengers to a range of 300 miles; and a few French Alouette III Astazous, which carry six people up to 375 miles.

The next step was to devise a plan to gain access to the makers concerned. As with all weapons of war there was a market – buyers, sellers and middlemen. Collins's business would make an ideal cover. He was known as a dealer to numerous auctioneers via the Home Office and his credentials were valid. The French make should not present a problem, but it was possible that he would have to go through a US dealer to reach the American helicopters. It might be expensive to gain access, let alone arrange for tuition.

* * *

Collins arrived at Cromer's town house that evening shortly before 9 p.m. As he swirled a Courvoisier around his brandy glass, he explained the plan.

'So to get out, yes, we use the helicopter. The problem was the make. Now I know they have two types. There's a strong possibility they will use an American Bell. They got a few as part of a deal with the USA four years ago. There is even a chance they'll use French Alouettes. We don't want to trust to luck. Two of us – Rourke and myself – have flying licences, but we don't want to be wondering where the starter button is when the Ethiopians come at us. We want to retrain with both makes. We can use the company as cover. I'll say I'm thinking of extending into military aircraft. I'll go to the RAF, the US Army, or the suppliers. Give me a few days – I think I should be able to arrange the flights.

'But it may cost money. We have to cut corners. I may even have to put a deposit on one or both of them. So I need your authority to spend anything up to £50,000, which I certainly don't have in the company. It may not happen, but I need the freedom.'

Cromer sipped his brandy and nodded. The costs were rising: £300,000 for Collins and his associates. Expenses to date: about £5000. Now, possibly £50,000 for the helicopters. Total so far: heading up towards half a million, and some way to go yet. He had no intention of spending anything like that much if he could help it, but to say so would be out of the question. Collins, Rourke and Halloran had to be confident they would return, at least in theory, otherwise they would never go.

'OK, Dicky,' said Cromer, 'go on.'

'Next problem: we plan to head for Kenya. It's English-speaking with good contacts back here, both vital as soon as we get over the border. We can assume the helicopter will have enough fuel to take Selassie back to Harar. But it's unlikely to have enough to get to the Kenyan border. We need a dump of fuel in Ethiopia. It will mean hiring a plane or helicopter in Nairobi and getting the stuff 100 miles or so over the border and hiding it. It may take a few days of Rourke's time and might cost another £3000 or so. He'll need to draw cash in Nairobi.'

'Again, OK.'

Collins knew he was taking a slight risk. Cromer might decide to back out. But, while driving down, he had become increasingly certain this wouldn't happen. Cromer was in too deep. Besides, far better that he had time now to decide on a strategy, than be shocked into a panic reaction later when plans were fully laid.

As it happened, Cromer had in the meantime devoted more thought to the problem than Collins. He had needed Collins's confirmation before developing his own plans further.

'Christ knows what the Ethiopians will do when they realize what's happened,' Collins concluded. 'Shouldn't like to be in your shoes.'

Cromer paused.

'It's all right, Dicky. I have every hope that they will swallow their anger. It will certainly be in their interests to do so. After all, we shall then be in a very favourable position to offer them a generous loan at remarkably advantageous rates of interest.'

Collins smiled. 'You always were a sly bastard, Charlie.'

Tuesday, 30 March
Collins began early to trace the machines he needed.

His first call to the Army Air Corps, at Middle Wallop, Wiltshire, brought both good news and bad. The good news was that the unit of 180 men whose job it was to turn out pilots for the Army could indeed lay its hands on an Alouette if needed (although the Army mostly used Gazelles). The bad news was that his former SAS status meant damn all.

Sorry, old boy, but the old boy network had all gone now. All very carefully accounted. These were expensive machines. More than the job's worth to slip outsiders into a retraining programme. A week? Good God, the minimum for retraining was two months. 'Besides,' the voice on the line concluded cheerily. 'There's the age factor. I'll bet you chaps wouldn't even get past the medical. Not that you'd notice in Civvy Street, but if you've seen active service you're probably half deaf. Even if you pass it'll take you sixty hours to requalify.'

Collins tried another tack. Anything for sale?

'Not a hope. The price of things nowadays, we repair everything. Some of the machines we have here are twenty, twenty-five years old. You'd have to buy new, straight from the French.'

Frustrated, Collins decided to try the American helicopters. A call to the Defence Attaché at the US Embassy led him back to the Army Air Corps, to an American exchange officer who proved a model of co-operation. The UH-IH had been used extensively in Vietnam as a combat troop carrier. They didn't carry many men, usually less than a dozen-man squad in 'Nam's hot, low-density air. But what the hell, at $250,000 they had been cheaper than the Chinooks, which held thirty-three. Boy, you get one of those hit by an RPG, and your costs really go through the roof. So, sure, the UHs were useful for 'ash-and-trash' work, food, medivac – all that stuff. But mostly for search-and-destroy missions – couple of pilots, crew chief who doubled as door-gunner, second door-gunner, couple of M60s. Handy little machines. Still use them at home for replacing crews at remote Minutemen missile-control centres.

'Here? Hell no, sir, we don't have any here. They're not licensed in this country. You'd have to go Stateside for one of those babies. You want to retrain? You could, I guess, at Fort Rucker, Alabama. But it would take you twenty-five hours' flying time. That'll take you, oh, twenty days minimum. That's without avionics training. Took me nine months to get out of that place . . . Buying, sure that'd be your best bet. Contact Bell Textron, they have a training base at Fort Worth, Texas, and they sell the whole deal: chopper, training programme, equipment, the lot. That's what the Iranians go for . . . Sure, sir, glad to be of service.'

Two dead ends. What about civil aviation schools? Surely they had machines? He called the AAC again.

'Well,' said the major to whom he had spoken a few minutes before. 'You might try Mark Winterton over at Kidlington. He's in the helicopter business. Perhaps he can help.'

He might have guessed: you phone the world, and then find what you want on your doorstep. And an individual. Must be better than an organization.

Winterton ran a helicopter hire business. Film, tanker crews, race meetings, he told Collins, anything that needs helicopters. Collins explained his problem, and Winterton rose to the challenge with zest.

Alouettes? Oh yes, quite common in civilian use. Used a good deal as camera platforms for film-making. Did Collins see *The Longest Day*, or *The Blue Max* or *The Battle of Britain*? Remember that terrific shot in *The Longest Day* after landing, which goes on for ever as some of our chaps fight their way along a canal side? Winterton had helped shoot it from an Alouette. And then, at last, the words Collins had been waiting to hear: 'Yes, I could get you into one.'

Collins detailed his requirements yet again and ended by saying: 'I know the rules. But don't they get bent?'

'Of course, all the time,' Winterton told him. 'Twenty-five hours is ideal for retraining. But it's your money. If you want a crash course, you could cut a few corners and fit the whole thing into a few days. That suit you? Fine. Leave it with me. I'll be back to you. Oh, yes, the cost may shock you: £200 per hour.'

The Bells were still a problem. Did he know anything about them?

'Funny thing about the Bells,' went on Winterton, who clearly enjoyed revealing his knowledge and experience. 'At the height of the Vietnam war, they were made under licence in Taiwan – not too reliably. When the Yanks went home they threw a few hundred into the seas. Literally tossed them overboard. But the Chinese went on building them anyway for a bit, and some of them finished up in pretty odd places. Rhodesia got some. Anyway, I think you'd have to go to the States for them, unless they sell them on the continent.'

Well, some progress. He'd try Bell direct in the afternoon.

At five o'clock, when the businesses in Texas would be well into their day, Collins called Bell in Fort Worth. To his relief there would be no point in a trip to the States. A drawling voice from the Training Programmes department told him that Bell itself trained only on the purchase of an aircraft. Sure, the military trained its personnel, but there would be a real problem getting in on that as a civilian. And that applied anywhere – no point going to Germany, for instance, where the Bundeswehr, the Luftwaffe and the Border Control all had military versions of Bells.

'But you know we have a commercial version of the UH-IH? It's designation is 205A-1, but if you find yourself a 205 or

206 you won't have any problem with a UH-IH . . . Yeah, sure we export them, that's our business . . . Yeah, I have a book here. We don't have anyone in England, but, why, we have half a dozen companies in Europe take Bell 205s.'

Collins scribbled down a list of names in Norway, Sweden, Holland and Austria. Holland: that should be possible.

'Yeah. I guess so. That's a commercial airline. They have retraining programmes of their own . . . Why, no trouble at all. Glad to be of service, sir.'

By the time the call ended, it was nearing six. Holland was one hour ahead. They'd be closed.

There was one further call a few minutes later: Winterton confirming he could offer a rapid retraining flight on an Alouette at Kidlington in the week beginning 12 April. Yes, he could pack twenty hours into two days. Gruelling, but possible, if Collins could meet the price: £7000 including tuition, helicopter hire and insurance. Fuel would be extra – perhaps another £500.

The Dutch company, Schreyver Airways, was as amenable to Collins's suggestion as Winterton had been. They were based at The Hague, had several 205s, and were happy to provide a one-day conversion course, for twice the price. They needed telexed confirmation and a ten per cent deposit, but otherwise no problems.

With his own plans all but laid for the helicopter training course, Collins turned his mind to another problem: Halloran. At that moment, he and Rourke were again studying the maps Rourke had picked up in Oxford. But Rourke could set up the fuel dumps on his own – he would be reliable enough, and space in the aircraft would be at a premium. Halloran would be left kicking his heels, with no real purpose over the next few days. It wasn't a good prospect. As the episode with the pheasants had shown, he was not totally reliable, except when he went into action. But there was no alternative. Better out here, in the depths of the country, where Collins could keep an eye on him, than sitting in some hotel room in London.

6

Wednesday, 31 March
Yufru called Cromer to arrange a meeting for midday. He
was excited: he had had a reply from the Emperor. When he
arrived, he set his briefcase on the glass-topped table, threw
himself into his now accustomed sofa and spread his arms
along its rich leather back.

'Sir Charles, this is high drama indeed. Let me tell you.
Your letter arrived yesterday afternoon. I had a car waiting
with my courier in it. I thought of taking the letter myself,
but . . . anyway, he travelled via Paris and took an overnight
flight to Addis via Rome, arriving early this morning . . .'

'Mr Yufru, the letter,' interrupted Cromer.

'Ah, yes. The Emperor dictated a reply in Amharic. I am
told he seemed to be his old self, still quite capable of decisive
thinking when necessary. At eighty-five! Remarkable . . .'

'The letter!'

'Ah, yes. It was helicoptered to Addis, translated into
English, and telexed back to me. A triumph, Sir Charles.'
He unclicked the briefcase and handed over the folded sheet.
Sir Charles sat back and read the four paragraphs.

'Sir Charles Cromer,

'Your letter has brought Us joy, and We have thought well on it. Our time is near and though Our Kingdom has been torn from Us by atheists, We are Father still to Our country and to Our family. Patiently enduring and making the faith We have in God the basis of all, We believe Our family must one day assume Our burdens, when the present times of difficulty are over. Their destiny is clear, and it is Our duty to ensure their return. To this end, they must live as Kings and Princes. A man cannot be loved as a Prince and live as a beggar. Therefore, We have decided to bestow upon Our sons and daughters the blessings that were once Ours.

'Sir Charles, We take note of your advice, as We once took note of your father's. This cannot be without the compliance of the present government. So be it.

'We therefore order you to prepare the documents necessary and to submit them for Our approval. God grant Us life until we meet, for We stand at the doors of death!'

Cromer let out a brief sigh of satisfaction, smiled briefly and laid the letter on the sofa beside him.

'You have succeeded, Sir Charles, where we have failed. You have our gratitude.'

'Spare me your thanks, Mr Yufru. We have much work to do. I must write again to the Emperor stating how exactly I suggest we dispose of his assets. We will then prepare a memorandum, including the Emperor's assets, that will act as a basis for the agreement. That document in its turn must be drawn up ready for signature by myself, my colleagues, your government, and by the Emperor. Yes, Mr Yufru, we still have much to do.'

'And I will wait. The only matter I must deal with rapidly is your delegation's entry visas. These are, of course, mere formalities. I will simply need from you application forms, filled in, in duplicate, with passport photos.'

Cromer felt a sudden qualm.

'But I take it you do not require the actual passports? My staff are busy, and may need to travel elsewhere before coming to Addis.'

'Well, in the circumstances, Sir Charles, the visas can be issued separately from the passports.'

The letter Cromer dictated to Valerie that afternoon he had carefully planned the previous evening. He modified it only slightly to take account of Selassie's response. Otherwise he preserved what was, in its way, a masterpiece of diplomacy, appealing both to the Emperor and the government.

He briefly reviewed Selassie's wealth and promised the details as soon as they were available. He was, he said, not concerned with actual quantities at present, though he guessed the total amount to be released exceeded $2000 million. He suggested a three-way division: eighty per cent to the government, fifteen per cent to Selassie's family and five per cent to the special account set aside for His Highness in case his situation should change. He concluded with a justification for this distribution, which was bound at first sight to seem to favour a government intent on wasting billions on wars, bribes and lavish buildings.

'Your Highness,

'You say you wish your family to live in comfort. But I beg you to consider that several hundred million dollars is enough for any family to live on, however great their previous expectations.

'I beg you furthermore to consider your country. Your countrymen are surely as much your family as your own offspring. If your wealth is to be distributed, should not your nation receive the predominant share?'

107

The five per cent special fund was a good touch; it was designed to suggest that, in exchange for his signature, the Emperor might be allowed to spend his days in comfortable exile. Cromer dictated a covering note to Yufru explaining his thinking, adding that if his government sought more than an eighty per cent share, Selassie might refuse the whole deal.

That afternoon he received two phone calls. The first was from Kupferbach in Zurich to say that the Swiss Foreign Office was not in principle against the use of the Swiss Embassy in Addis on a matter of such supreme national importance. Kupferbach said he was attending a meeting in the ministry on Monday to explain personally that this would be the least the country could do, since it meant retaining in Switzerland several hundred million dollars.

The second call was from Collins, to say that he would take Rourke to Heathrow for his flight to Nairobi the following afternoon.

Thursday, 1 April
During the course of the morning, two couriers arrived with deliveries for Cromer: one from New York, the other from Zurich. It was surprising to him that there were men prepared to spend their lives in aeroplanes, but it was a godsend at times like this. Each package contained a portfolio of several pages: Selassie's holdings. His own bank's statement also lay before him.

New York's was by far the most complex of the three. It had been on Cromer's father's advice in 1948 that Selassie had begun diversifying his wealth, placing a good deal of it on the other side of the Atlantic. It had been an astute move. Gold from Zurich, at that time selling for $35 an ounce, had been used to buy a spread of stocks amounting to $100 million over ten years. In the following two decades, those stocks, carefully nurtured by Lodge's people, had grown along with the American economy at an average of between five and ten per cent per year and now totalled almost $1000 million. Cromer was always copied on purchases and sales, but he'd never seen the portfolio summarized and assessed in this way.

Then there were companies in which the Emperor was a sleeping partner: a property company in Dallas, a clothing manufacturer in New Jersey, an art gallery in New York – eleven in all, reflecting a passing passion or advice taken or favour given. To liquidate the arrangements would be difficult – perhaps disastrous for the companies concerned and certainly expensive in legal fees.

There was also the gold held directly by the Federal Reserve Bank of New York at Liberty Street. It represented a 100-ton shipment that arrived from London and Zurich in 1939, when Europe was preparing for war. Now, with gold standing at $173 an ounce, it was worth just over $800 million – which was, noted Cromer, a considerably less substantial increase proportionately than the increase in the value of the stocks.

The Zurich statement was simpler. Much of it confirmed what he already knew, for the Swiss gold, though shown to the Emperor's credit in Zurich, had in fact been left in the London vaults, simply out of convenience. This was not an unusual situation. As often with gold (like that from South Africa) it had been transported under arrangements of proven security for many decades and it was simpler to keep it in London, even if it was to be credited in Switzerland. The Swiss banks simply paid a handling and rental charge. A considerable sum had, however, been air-freighted directly to Zurich in recent years. Finally, Zurich also held the Maria Theresa dollars, air-freighted there in the 1940s.

From all three centres there were details of currency accounts which were held for immediate settlements – for cars, works of art, horses, furniture, clothing, anything the Emperor had needed from abroad for himself or his family.

Cromer jotted down the main figures, and tapped them into a calculator.

The grand total was just short of $3000 million.

Friday, 2 April
Rourke arrived in Nairobi that morning after an eight-hour flight. He took a rattling cab from Embakasi International Airport, through the capital – spacious, if strangely lifeless after London – to the Hilton, a twenty-storey cylinder that towers over the glass and concrete of central Nairobi on the corner of Mama Ngina Street and Government Road.

Exhausted from a night of fitful napping, he nevertheless began a series of calls to track down a company that flew helicopters. He spoke to two wildlife groups and a film unit, none of whom could or would help; his fourth attempt, after three-quarters of an hour, struck lucky. The company was called Autoflight and they had a number of planes for hire. He said he wanted helicopters, as soon as possible, to take some equipment north 'to the Ethiopian border'. Yes, said a male voice claiming to belong to an individual named Swain, yes, in theory they could do it; and yes, they could even do it immediately if given a good reason, by which Rourke understood them to mean a lot of money. He suggested a more detailed discussion and was invited to the offices at Nairobi's general aviation airport, Wilson Airfield.

His cab found the place after twenty minutes, back out towards Embakasi. There, in a concrete hut beside a couple of hangars emblazoned with the company's name, he found a man

110

and a woman. Chris Swain was in his mid-forties and dressed in a short-sleeved shirt that hung loosely over his blue slacks. He wore sneakers. He was small, with startling blue eyes and a clipped dark beard. Though Rourke never knew his background, he had in fact been a schoolmaster in England before coming to Africa one summer fifteen year earlier. He had taken a temporary job with Autoflight and never returned home. He learned flying, loved it, eventually took over the business and built it up to its present level: two fixed-wings and two helicopters. Most of his business came from tourists and wildlife management people, contract work with game parks and companies wanting to get people across East Africa in a hurry. One of the monoplanes was out now, and so was one of the helicopters.

'Rourke?' he said matter of factly, 'Swain. How do you do. My wife, Judy, Mr Rourke.'

Judy, originally Judith, was of German extraction. She also wore slacks. She was taller than her husband, and ten years younger, with a mass of blonde curls. Like him, she gave the impression of directness, of physical hardness. She too flew. Her parents had been born in German East Africa, and when she was twenty had made a sentimental journey to show her the place. In Dar es Salaam she had met Chris, been fascinated by his driving intensity and his neat good looks, and had run away with him.

Rourke put his proposition straight, without giving any explanation: he wanted to place enough fuel somewhere up by Lake Chamo, to get either a Bell UH-IH or an Alouette from there back down to Nairobi. He also wanted to be shown a route that was impossible to lose.

Swain raised his eyebrows.

'Ethiopia,' he said. 'I take it you don't wish to apply for a visa and flying permissions? No, I thought not. Well, that

111

simplifies things . . . Alouettes I know. Or a Bell UH-IH? They're the 205-As, commercial designation? Good, tough machines. We have JetRangers.'

He sniffed, sat down and pulled out some grubby maps from under a pile of papers on his desk.

'The filing system,' he said, 'we're flyers here. Try to keep things in order, but the work keeps getting in the way . . . Ah, Chamo.'

He checked some distances with a pencil. 'Yes, quite a way. Five hundred miles. You know the range of your machines? Yes, a touch over three hundred. OK, let's see what's involved.'

It turned out that a great deal was involved. Assuming their helicopter was empty at Chamo, Rourke, Collins and Halloran would need access to a minimum of 350 US gallons of fuel; nine forty-five-gallon drums to be on the safe side. Neither the Bell nor the Alouette held that much in its tank, so they would have to establish two, perhaps three dumps *en route*.

Next, where to place the fuel and how to get it there. Swain's JetRangers couldn't do it all. They would have to have a truck, and use a JetRanger as well. Swain started scribbling on a bit of paper, cross-correlating weights, distances and fuel consumption. Eventually he concluded: 'Shame you need to have a clear route. You could just follow the radio beacons. You simply dial in the frequencies and the aircraft homes in on its ADF – automatic direction-finder.'

'Yeah. I remember.'

'OK, then. How about coming straight down, across country?' Swain slid a finger across the map south from Lake Chamo.

'What's the country like?'

'Terrible. Featureless. Lava and sand. But you could follow the beacons, then the Nairobi-Addis Highway. It's metalled from somewhere inside the Ethiopian border.'

'But not all the way?'

'No . . .'

'Don't like the sound of it. Besides, I might not be the pilot. The Rift Valley route looks easy.'

'It is. Longer, but you can't get lost. Lakes. Volcanoes. Clear as anything. Now let's see where we make the dumps.'

It turned out that the truck Swain said he could use – a four-wheel-drive Bedford belonging to a local safari company – would have to set out with twenty drums. It would drop seven drums at the Kampi ya Samaki ('Camp of Fish') airstrip at Lake Baringo, then head north 200 miles to the eastern shores of Lake Rudolf, to a desolate headland of lava hills called Kobi Fora. There it would leave fifteen drums.

Following a day later with Rourke, the JetRanger would refuel at Lake Baringo, and again at Kobi Fora, where it would also pick up four drums and ferry them up to Chamo.

'Not that you'll need all four,' said Swain, 'but it's useful to have a reserve.'

Having made its drop, the JetRanger would then head south again, refuelling *en route*. When Rourke, Collins and Halloran came south in their turn . . .

'How do we find our way?' Rourke interrupted.

'You follow the Rift.'

'I mean when we leave Addis.'

'It's as easy down from Addis as it is north of here. Look at the map. There are lakes all the way and the walls on either side guide you like a tunnel. You won't even need the beacon at Arba Minch . . . Anyway, when you come south, you will have two dumps. You'll see them both on the way tomorrow. Back here the day after, and home on the overnight flight. OK?'

'Sounds good – if you can get the truck.'

113

'Shouldn't be a problem. There's lots of trucks and labour. We need two drivers and a camp boy. I've got the fuel. But I may have to offer extra for immediate action.'

'Sure.'

'Right. I'll let you know if there're any problems. But we've done this sort of thing before. Survey work, we say. That covers a multitude of sins . . . You'll be flying with my other pilot, young chap called Bob Hudson. He knows all about the Rift. The only thing that'll stop you is the price.'

He did more sums. Nine hundred gallons of fuel at seven Kenyan shillings per gallon. The truck, plus three men. The JetRanger for two days, plus pilot, at £200 per hour. Total: just short of £4000.

In cash.

Rourke sighed. He didn't have the cash and he wasn't authorized to draw that much anyway. He could phone Collins, who could phone Cromer, who could authorize a bank draft. Swain accepted that idea.

'If anything goes wrong,' Swain concluded, 'I'll bloody well fly back up to Chamo and put a bullet through your bloody drums myself.'

He then relented a little and over a beer and sandwiches told Rourke something about Hudson, a young geologist whose passion for the Rift Valley and for photography had led him to the Swains. He had taken a civilian flying course in England and found that the only way he could indulge his consuming interests was by hiring himself out as a pilot.

'He won't be in today,' said Swain. 'But he'll have to come in tomorrow to get things ready. He knows the place better than I do. He can explain all you'll need to remember.'

That afternoon, Rourke returned, drawn with tiredness and heat, to the sanctuary of his air-conditioned hotel room to make his calls, to have a bath, and to sleep.

Selassie's reply, duly translated as before, arrived on Cromer's desk that morning. The Emperor was apparently resigned to the dissipation of his fortune, and had accepted without question Cromer's suggestions. His only stipulation was the release from house arrest of a number of relatives. To this, the Ethiopians had apparently agreed.

Cromer thought the time might be right for a turn of the screw. There must be no backtracking now by the Ethiopians. He wanted to wind up their expectations at once and irreversibly. Before he began the arduous task of drafting the memorandum detailing the division of the imperial spoils he called Yufru.

'Mr Yufru,' began Cromer, 'I have before me both the Emperor's favourable reply to my proposals and an assessment of his holdings world-wide. It may be of interest for you to know that, all being well, your government is likely to be richer very shortly by over $2000 million.'

There was a long silence, then Yufru said: 'Sir Charles, I will inform the powers that be. I should like you to know that if this transaction is completed successfully, Ethiopia will be eternally in your debt. It may quite literally save the country from disaster. Moreover it may well be that with such a sum we shall buy what we need and keep ourselves independent, clear of the clutches of the Soviet Union. Your actions, Sir Charles, will change the course of African history.'

'Oh, come, Mr Yufru, no need for that,' Cromer said, deprecating, magnanimous. 'I shall now draw up the memorandum of transfer and will contact you later.'

The memorandum of transfer. It sounded suitably formal and imposing as a title for the document he then began to draft. It was an intricate piece of work, summarizing how the sums were to be realized: the sale of the gold on the open market, the sale of the shares, the liquidation of the company holdings. There were clauses on the transfer of the sums to local branches of the Bank of Ethiopia, the legal problems likely to be encountered with the companies, the question of taxation, the involvement of the Bank of England and Federal Reserve, both of whom would need to be informed – a myriad of details designed to create the impression of a masterly balance between the conflicting demands of haste and realism, all the convincing detail of a document designed to be nothing but a perfect smokescreen.

After three hours Cromer began to edit his work, cutting here, adding there, swinging paragraphs into a more logical sequence. That afternoon – after dealing with a few urgent letters – he began to dictate a draft of the memorandum, a 3000-word statement that would act as the basis for comments, firstly from Zurich and New York, secondly from Addis and thirdly (possibly) from Selassie himself.

Saturday, 3 April
Before take-off from Nairobi, the twenty-six-year-old pilot, Bob Hudson, briefed Rourke about the geography of the Rift Valley. He turned out to be effusive, even over-effusive, about his subject. He had a kinked nose (the result of a rugger injury), and a habit of pulling his top lip back from his teeth when embarrassed. His hearty public-school accent grated constantly on Rourke.

'Look at the map, here,' Hudson said. 'Here's the Rift just outside Nairobi. The walls go up northwards on either side here and here. They spread out as they go past Lake Rudolf, which is where we're heading, and then together again, up through Ethiopia. But the centre's always marked by lakes and volcanoes. Funny place. You know why?'

Rourke gave him no encouragement. Undeterred, Hudson put his hands together in a position as if for prayer, except tilted over, and as he talked they fell apart to dramatize his words. 'The whole of East Africa and Arabia is being torn apart, sort of unzipped, along the line of the Rift. As the sides pulled apart, the middle bit fell. All sorts of things seep up from below – lava and soda mainly – so the landscapes are often all twisted and the lakes are white and salty-looking with soda deposits round the edge. You'll see. Sometime, millions of years hence, this place will be on another continent and over there, westwards, the other side of those hills, there'll be a new strip of ocean. Fabulous thought, isn't it?'

'Uh huh,' said Rourke, unmoved. 'How do I recognize . . .?'

'Well, first you'll see the edge of the Rift . . .' said Hudson, and went on to brief Rourke in rather more detail with the aid of the map. It took half an hour. They were ready to leave shortly after nine o'clock.

The JetRanger was standing on a concrete square thirty yards away from the shed. They climbed in, with Rourke in the second pilot's seat, and fixed seat belts and headsets.

Hudson said: 'Here, take the map. You'll see the way.' He made his take-off checks and pushed the starter button to ignite the turbine.

The helicopter thumped into life, hauled itself slowly aloft towards the haze that precedes the Kenyan rains, and bent away north and west, swinging over Uhuru Park and out above the dual carriageway of Uhuru Avenue. Rourke gave the broad streets and well-spaced buildings not a second glance, straining forward instead to familiarize himself with the geography of the place, which he would have to recall well enough to bring Collins and Halloran on their flight from Addis Ababa.

As the machine picked up its cruising speed of 130 m.p.h., the town fell away behind them. Buildings and roads gave way to patchwork patterns of banana and vegetable plantations, which were in their turn replaced by forest. Suddenly, after fifteen minutes, the ground rose slightly and then dropped away over 2000 feet to savannah and grasslands.

'The Rift!' said Hudson. Then, as he swung north to follow the line of the hills, he pointed out to the left. There, blue and hazy some twenty miles away on the other side of the Rift, was the Mau Escarpment.

Beating northwards, Hudson shouted out the landmarks. Longonot, its dormant one-mile-wide crater blanketed with forest. Lake Naivasha, its fresh water teeming with birds and fish. Lake Nakuru, with its red and white swirls of flamingos. On Nakuru's shores, almost invisible in the yellow grasses, a herd of zebra scattered, spooked by the noise of the helicopter.

Half an hour later, 'Baringo!' said Hudson. 'Lots of crocs!'

He set the JetRanger down on the edge of the strip by the single hangar. There was no one else there. The drums awaited them. Hudson removed a toggle-pump from the rear compartment. The two of them manhandled two drums, weighing 300lb apiece, over to the helicopter, and pumped in their contents, an operation that with the fast-action pump took less than fifteen minutes. They were airborne again within half an hour of landing.

Now there would be a longer gap as the Rift walls fell away almost to invisibility on either side, and the grasses died back to form a parched and desolate landscape of sparse scrub over volcanic rock.

'Heading due north!' said Hudson, pointing at the compass. 'Hit Rudolf one hour after Baringo. Keep an eye on speed and time.'

After that he said little until Lake Rudolf appeared as a narrow sliver ahead. It was at that moment an extraordinary green, the result of algae blooming in its acrid waters, a regular phenomenon that had given the lake its nickname, the Jade Sea. Hudson swung along the lake's eastern edge, up the coast along a pile of crumpled volcanic hills and over a lava plain until a collection of huts rolled towards them. A dusty airstrip ran alongside the huts. A truck was parked nearby.

Hudson put the helicopter down by a shack and as the engine died away an emaciated black came out, wearing tattered trousers and a dirty shirt. A few goats wandered the barren hills, tearing at the scanty plants. Rourke grimaced at the heat and the drabness.

Hudson noticed his expression. 'Bit rough, you think? Not a bit, old boy. This man has class. You should see the others. Stark naked. Probably out fishing.'

They had meanwhile been joined by three other blacks, likewise dressed in open shirts and filthy trousers. They were the crew of the truck. Hudson spoke to them in Swahili. They wandered back to the truck and began to unload the drums. Once again, Rourke and Hudson refuelled. Then from the rear of the truck appeared a net.

Hudson shouted. After another few minutes, the cargo net was established alongside the JetRanger, wrapped around four drums. While Hudson pulled out a line and hook from beneath the aircraft, and proceeded to attach the hook to the top of the net, Rourke surveyed the grim landscape. The place looked as if it had been newly fired in some giant kiln. Towards the lakeside, a few gnarled trees scrabbled for a toe-hold on the lava, bent all about with the effort of growth. Here and there, tussocks of dry grass provided the only other relief from the rocks, grey sand and lava dust. In the distance, hazy behind little whirls of dust whipped up by the hot wind, precipitous crags plunged down to the water's edge. Hudson looked up, wiped his brow and followed Rourke's gaze.

'Barren as hell. And largely because of those damn animals.' He pointed to the goats. 'They pull everything up by the roots. Anyway, walk around if you like. Watch out for snakes. I had a mamba in my rucksack once.'

It was midday and fearfully hot. The wind had risen and was battering their shirts against their bodies. Hudson signalled Rourke into the JetRanger, and said: 'Drink?'

Rourke hadn't appreciated just how dehydrated he'd become and downed a pint of water without pausing. Hudson had sandwiches. The two of them ate.

'Jesus,' Rourke said, 'what a bloody place.'

'Beautiful, often, actually,' said Hudson, 'and very important. Not long ago, Richard Leakey found a fossilized human skull about three million . . . oh, forget it. Sorry,' he said, seeing Rourke glance at his watch. 'All right. Let me have another drink and we'll move.'

Before take-off, in the helicopter, Hudson opened the map again to show Rourke the final leg of their outward journey. At the tip of Lake Rudolf, another 100 miles north, they would swing east over Lake Stephanie, then up towards the Ethiopian section of the Rift, and their destination, Lake Chamo.

'Won't we be spotted?'

'Possibly. Probably. But there's nothing to worry about. There are one or two civilian airstrips, but no military bases. No one's going to follow us. Where we land, there are no roads and damn few people. We take care, of course. We won't be there more than an hour or so.'

They prepared for departure. This time Hudson took the machine up slowly, edged it across above the cargo net, and when he was directly above, continued to ascend slowly until the line went taut and he saw his cargo was safely aloft.

They headed north along the shoreline over the appalling landscape. Then Hudson swung away eastwards.

'The border!' he said after half an hour. Below, Rourke could see a line created by bush-clearance. That was all there was to it. Where there was no vegetation, there was no line. An open border.

North and east of Lake Rudolf, the ground rolled up into rocky hills in which lay a sheet of water: Lake Stephanie, so shallow that it varies from a puddle to a swamp to a ten-mile lake from month to month, depending on the rainfall. Flamingos. Zebra drumming in herds over the open areas. Green sedge marshes where a river from the north evaporated. Mud flats. Rolling grasslands leading to uplands. Then finally, Lake Chamo, twenty miles long, and to the north just visible beyond a forested hump of hills, its sister, Lake Abaya.

Hudson set the helicopter down on the southern shores of the lake back from the pebbly waterside, near a defile made by a stream running down from high ground to the east. As the machine settled beside its cargo, the slapping rotors swished into silence and the scattering of low trees that marked the defile became still. Below them and to their right, reeds and rushes marked the confluence of stream and lake. The reeds were swaying and the sound of splashing came up to them.

'Hippo!' said Hudson, happily.

He had chosen the spot well. He unhooked the cargo net, and the two of them rolled the drums a few yards uphill to a group of thorn bushes. From ten yards away, they couldn't be seen.

Rourke looked around. A marabou stork strutted from the shallows, black wing-tips meeting over its back like a gowned professor. Yes, the spot was identifiable enough. The southern shore was a sweep about ten miles long. Much of it was a repetition of reeds and pebbles, but to their right, beyond the defile, a river came into the lake. Rourke took the pad and a pencil, strolled a couple of hundred yards towards it and made a quick sketch of the geography.

As he strolled back, Hudson called: 'Hey, come on!' and then, as he got closer: 'It's 3.30! We want to get back before nightfall. Besides, if anyone saw us come down, someone, somewhere is going to talk. We don't want visitors to find us still around.'

'I thought you said no one lived here.'

'Well, the lake is fished. And there are herders.'

He offered Rourke a drink from his water-flask and they prepared for take-off.

'Oh, one last thing,' said Hudson, 'getting down here I told you it's 250 miles. You'll be OK, if you just come south between the escarpments. That's the southern tip of them,' he said, pointing to hills to the west. 'The lakes will guide you. Now, let's get out of here.'

Kupferbach woke Cromer with a call to his home at 7.10 a.m.

'Charles? I am sorry to call you at this hour, but I wanted you to know that I have seen our Foreign Minister last night. Are you awake? Shall I call back later?'

'No, Oswald, tell me now.'

'Very well. He will inform the Embassy in Addis that the building must be cleared on Sunday 11 April. The Ambassador alone will know why. You must provide details of what else is required – conference facilities, seating plan, food, papers, and so on. He will be there to hand over the building to your people. Then he will drive away.'

'Finally, I asked for plans. We are a most efficient people, Charles. In the Foreign Office, they have plans of all our embassies, all around the world. It is necessary to have such details in case of the need to escape or to withstand a siege. He has ordered the plans to be copied. They will be with me on Monday.'

7

Monday, 5 April

Collins started selling off his stock. When Stan asked him about it, he said: 'Profits are getting squeezed, Stan. We'll just cut down on costs for a month or two until we see how things shape up.'

Cromer phoned Collins, informed him that the plans had arrived and told him to get down the following day. Collins had, in his turn, told Cromer that Rourke had made the fuel drop and that he would pick him up at Heathrow the following morning, on his way into town.

Tuesday, 6 April

When Collins and Halloran met Rourke early the following morning, they found him in remarkably good shape. He had slept for most of the overnight flight and was largely recovered from his gruelling experience.

At first he said little, but driving into London he told the story at some length.

'I've no doubts about getting south from Chamo,' he finished. 'You could do it simply enough without any preparation. You were right about the Rift: it is easy to follow. We just have to make sure we recognize Chamo when we approach from the north. I've made a sketch of where the fuel is.'

'Confident?' asked Collins.

'No trouble,' Rourke replied with a grin. 'Once we get to Chamo, our troubles will be over.'

In town, Collins told Rourke and Halloran to book a room in the Hilton as an HQ, while he saw Cromer.

He was with Cromer in his office at nine o'clock, even before Valerie had arrived. Cromer told him of the statements of the Emperor's holdings, the memorandum, the agreement of the Swiss to use the embassy and finally indicated the plans on the table between them.

Collins reached for the large envelope Cromer pushed across to him, and slid out the contents. Inside were four blueprint sheets, specifications for the Swiss Embassy in Addis Ababa: cellar, two floors and an overall scheme of the building in its compound. Each room was numbered and the numbers keyed to a list reproduced on the side on each sheet. Underneath the list was a scale.

'Perfect,' said Collins.

'We'll have copies made and you can study them. Let me know if there are any problems. Now, there are other reasons for you to be here. One is to start the business of accreditation. I'm going to need photographs of you three for visas. For those you won't need passports. But to travel you will. Can you arrange false passports for the others in a hurry?'

'Well, false passports are arranged often enough in the SAS, but I doubt if I can get them that way. Maybe we'll have to buy them.'

'How much?'

'No idea. A thousand pounds each? I daren't even guess. And the time element is tricky. Paper, inks, Christ knows what. I've no underworld contacts. Perhaps Halloran can help. You want me to call him?'

Outside, a desk drawer slammed. Valerie had arrived.

Cromer said: 'No, not now. Speak to him later. The other thing is that later this afternoon I'll have the first draft of the document on which the transaction will officially be based. You should all have one. You'll have to know it well. You are to be a gold expert, Dicky. I'll look out some of the background to Selassie's gold dealing over the years and copy them for you.'

'OK.'

'One more thing. Yufru is coming in to collect his copy of the memorandum today. Just a brief visit. I'd like you to meet him, but only in passing. We won't get into any long conversations and anyway, your role will be quite deferential. Any technical questions you can leave me to answer.'

'But I don't have an identity yet.'

'I thought I would introduce you as my deputy, name of Jeremy Squires. He's a bit younger than you, but if Yufru thinks to check up, he'll find that Squires's qualifications are perfect. I don't want any more deception in the office than that, or something's going to leak out. But I do want to keep Yufru's confidence in us at a high level. He's due at five. Come back then.'

Collins was with Rourke and Halloran half an hour later.

'One more thing,' he added, after briefing them. 'Do either of you know any way of getting forged passports?'

'Jesus,' said Halloran, 'a bit late for that. I assumed Cromer had that under control. Diplomatic status or some such.'

'Well, no. Sorry.'

'Forged passports . . . I've tried for that. It could solve a lot of my problems. New identity, no links with the past. Fuckin' business it is, in this civilized country. You have to be in Istanbul. Even there, it's a risk. Fifteen hundred quid is the going rate and there's no way you can check on die-stamps and paper quality, the things the immigration people here pick up on. Forget the forgeries, I say. It's easier to do it legal, that's what I was told, if you're British.'

'Legally?' said Collins. 'I'd better check up on that.'

He glanced at his watch. A quarter to one.

The three men ate in the hotel in order to lunch at Cromer's expense, before the next meeting.

There were a number of tasks still to be fitted in.

First, passport photos. That was solved with a visit to the shopping arcade beneath the hotel. Then came what they assumed would be the major problem of false identities. This turned out to be not as difficult as Collins feared. He called the Passport Office and said he was a Jewish businessman who needed to travel to North Africa. Was there any legal way to avoid being identified by his real name?

The reply was a revelation: 'Well, we don't wish to encourage deception, but lots of people need more than one passport, sometimes in different names. There's no great mystery. We're in the business of issuing passports, after all. If you fulfil the statutory requirements, you get the passport.'

'And the requirements are?'

'A visa application, two photos, details of previous passport. And new name, if different from the old.'

'A new name?'

'Well, most people think you can acquire a new name only by a deed poll. No, you can do it far more simply, with a Statutory

Declaration provided by a solicitor and sworn before a Commissioner of Oaths. The cost is £1.50, £2, no more. Why, sir, you could, in case of need, change your name and have a new passport all within two hours.'

It was as easy as it sounded. Collins called Cromer and obtained the name of a West End solicitor. On his way over to Cromer, Collins called in to the solicitor's office and was shown a copy of the standard change-of-name declaration, comic in its legalistic lack of punctuation and repetitiveness.

They could all get new names and new passports entirely legally, tomorrow.

Collins arrived back at Cromer's office shortly before five o'clock. Cromer's door was open, the outer office was empty.

'Charlie,' he said loudly.

Cromer called him in, told him to close the door and waved him to a sofa. 'Sent my secretary home,' he said. 'I didn't want her overhearing me talking about you as Jeremy Squires. Do you have anything?'

Collins told him about new passports, and handed over the photos for the visas.

'Here, take a look through this,' Cromer went on. 'Take three copies.'

On the table was a pile of half a dozen folders, each containing a score of photocopied pages: Cromer's memorandum and a three-page balance sheet of the Emperor's holdings.

'If the Emperor ever got to sign this, we'd all be ruined. It's the gold you should know about, almost £2000 million worth. There are a few personal fortunes worth more – the Shah's, the Hunt family in Texas, Howard Hughes – but none so concentrated now in the hands of one man, and none so easily assessed. You can imagine what would happen if we had to . . .'

The phone interrupted him. 'Excellent,' he said, answering. 'Ask him to come up, would you, Jim?' Then, as he put down the phone: 'Yufru. Get introduced and then make yourself scarce.'

Yufru, urbane as ever, bearing a wafer-thin briefcase, raised a supercilious eyebrow at Collins's presence when he strolled over from the lift.

'Ah, Mr Yufru. Let me introduce you to the senior member of my team, Jeremy Squires. Mr Squires is considered the expert in the Emperor's gold shares . . . Mr Squires, Mr Yufru, a representative of the Ethiopian government, and the vital link in all our negotiations.'

The two men shook hands. Yufru placed his case on Cromer's desk and clicked it open.

'Sir Charles, Mr Squires, I have four visa application forms I would like filled in. A mere formality. Simply return them to me, with pictures.'

Cromer glanced at the simple, cyclostyled sheets. Name, date of birth, profession, passport number. Straightforward enough.

'You don't need our passports?'

'No. I will simply have the correct stamps and signatures added, and return the forms to you.'

He glanced down at the folders held by Collins.

'Yes, Mr Yufru,' said Cromer, 'this is the treaty, and the statement of the holdings. The first draft, a document for discussion over the next few days. Er . . . Mr Squires?'

Collins took the cue.

'Yes, indeed, Sir Charles. I look forward to working with you, Mr Yufru. A challenge, a marvellous experience, I'm sure. Till later then.'

Collins left, surprised to find his heart racing at the success of this simple piece of deception.

Tuesday, 6 April
Collins, Rourke and Halloran followed through the rigmarole of acquiring new passports. First, more photographs. Next, a brief appointment with the same solicitor to fill in the Statutory Declaration. Then to a second solicitor, a Commissioner of Oaths – 'Yes, we have to send you next door, gentlemen, to avoid the possibility of fraud' – to swear to the truth of the document.

'You realize, of course, gentlemen,' said the solicitor, who was clearly used to the notion of people changing names, 'that should you for any reason wish in the future to be known once more by your previous name, you simply go through this little procedure again.'

Then to the Passport Office in Petty France to fill out application forms in their new names: Jeremy Squires, David Sackville-Jones, George Smithson. Collins gave Cromer as a reference, and spun a story about business needs – immediate action – leaving the next day – sensitive area – must have passports as soon as possible.

As they waited for Collins to return, Rourke said: 'You realize, Pete, the change will be on record? The police will get around to checking passport applications sooner or later.'

'But I'll be long gone, old son, won't I?'

'Hope so. Just thought I'd remind you.'

Collins walked back to them.

'They'll be ready at three. Let's sink a pint.'

Wednesday, 7 April
After an early breakfast, Collins and Rourke drove down towards Oxford for the first day of their training on the Alouette.

Kidlington Airport, which lies off the road linking Woodstock and Oxford, is used for private planes, for training in both fixed-wings and helicopters, and for sales. It was raining lightly as Collins guided the Range Rover between the scattering of offices, lecture rooms, workshops, and hangars to the building that housed Winterton's outfit. They found him with his feet on the table, browsing through sales pamphlets. He was a solid six-footer dressed in a blue Guernsey sweater and jeans.

Over coffee, Winterton probed Collins and Rourke for their flying experience over the last few years.

Rourke had a good head start: during his service in Oman he had flown a Scout and a Bell 47. He had behind him some 500 hours of flying experience, a good deal of it in windy and mountainous conditions in the Arabian peninsula. Flying the Alouette would present him with no great problem – five hours' experience should be enough – but with some intensive training on start-up procedures.

Collins's needs were greater. He had his Private Pilot's Licence and had fulfilled his statutory five hours of flying annually to keep his PPL current, but his experience was limited to piston engines. The Alouette was a turbine.

'At your age,' said Winterton rather unkindly, 'we have a problem with the fatigue factor. It's like playing the piano, learning a new machine. If you've never converted, just imagine the problems – external checks, internal checks, starting procedures for cold and hot engines, warm-up, ground checks, pre-take-off checks, after take-off checks – well, you probably remember what it was like. Anyway, 120 or more points to bear in mind, and that's without avionics training and emergency procedures . . . OK, OK' – he saw Collins's impatient expression – 'just reminding you that there's a limit to what I can force into you in one day. Mr Rourke – Michael – you'll come out all right. But, Major, I'd advise you not to fly unless you have to. You'll have the very, very basics . . . yes, enough to fly, but no more.'

Winterton's warnings turned to incredulity when Collins told him the other two complexities: they wanted to prepare for a rapid take-off at 8000 feet near the equator.

'Oh, my God, Major. The air's less dense by about a third at that height. And if it's hot, that's more difficult still. And you want a rapid take-off? You know in a turbine you can burn out an engine instantaneously if you get the balance between fuel and air wrong . . . Well, gentlemen, we have our work cut out. But I warn you it will be tough, with no guarantees. You're still game? OK, let's make a start. First I'll introduce you to the machine . . .'

He took them outside, through the slanting rain, to an Alouette standing on its cement square at the edge of the airfield.

'You won't remember anything in detail at this stage, but I'll just give you a feel of the problem,' he said over their shoulders as the two men settled into the dual-control pilots' seats, and clicked their belt-and-shoulder harness into place. 'Cyclic controls, throttle, collective pitch, pedals . . .'

So began a day of the most intensive training either man had ever experienced. Some of the time they were together on the ground, mainly learning to drill into themselves a sequence of checks that would cover the essential instruments in the minimum time. Rourke went up first, with Winterton sitting in beside him. For Collins, who was not to fly until later, the day became a timeless round of rote learning, until, at dusk, he was able to take the controls.

As they drove back exhausted, both knew that however far they fell short of a formal qualification, they would at least be able to get away from the embassy at short notice. What appalled them – and Collins in particular – was that within a few days they would have to repeat similarly demanding procedures with a totally different machine.

Back in the Hilton that evening, Collins and Rourke came to Halloran's room. Collins opened his briefcase, and produced the plans of the embassy, placing the ground-floor sheet on the coffee-table alongside the overall view of the compound.

'Distances. Doorways. Entrances. It looks clear enough. First thing: I think we stick to the ground floor. It makes for a quicker getaway, and Selassie might not be too good at stairs. That leaves only one real possibility. The left-hand rooms are out: they all seem set aside for routine embassy business: secretaries, visas, stuff like that. But here on the right is the main ambassadorial office, linked to some other large room. Doors all round. This is where we set things up . . .'

The three talked on, working out the details of the kidnapping. The conference to be held in the front office. The back office to be arranged for more informal discussions. Cromer could add the details – seating, refreshments, stationery – when he contacted Switzerland. The important thing was the geography of the place, and the order of events.

'You're right, Michael,' said Collins. 'We separate them, one at a time if possible, into the next-door room. I'll have to work out some way to break the conference, to get us in there in the first place. But it shouldn't be hard. I'll talk to Cromer about it tomorrow and we'll spot some weak link in the document. You'll have to leave the stage management to me. Then, Peter, we'll let you take over.'

Halloran smiled. 'One at a time. No problem at all.'

'We ought to make sure there are a few solid pieces of furniture,' Rourke suggested. 'A sofa or two. We don't want bodies

lying around in full view.' Collins rubbed his eyes to clear the
pricking tiredness. It was after 2.30 a.m.

'Couldn't really be better,' he said. 'A ten-foot wall, heavy
gates. We may have trouble with the guards, especially if
they're inside the gates. But if we're quiet, even that might
not be a problem. Then, after it's over, we grab the old man
and head for the helicopter, and hope we can get the damn
thing airborne before the guards realize what's going on.' He
yawned. 'God. Look at the time. We have to sleep, otherwise
Michael and I won't be good for anything in The Hague.'

Collins then went through the plan again, step by step,
minute by minute, and each man built the scene in his mind's
eye as he talked.

Friday, 9 April
If Collins and Rourke had later been asked to recall any
details of their day in Holland, they would scarcely have
been able to do so. They had taken an afternoon shuttle the
previous day from Heathrow to The Hague. Exhausted from
their near-sleepless night, they had booked into an airport
hotel and after a rapid supper of cold meat and salad,
collapsed into bed. Neither could have placed on a map the
airfield to which their cab took them in the morning. Their
attention, from the first five minutes of their arrival, was
directed towards the machine on which they were to train,
under the tuition of a dour Dutchman with too many teeth.

The Bell 205-A, like the Alouette, is a turbine, but it is a
much bigger machine. In America and Europe, it usually
carries up to fifteen people with its twin-bladed rotor. (In the
tropics and at altitude – in lower-density air – it carries less.)
Collins's brief in-flight experience in the Alouette was of some
use, but the major problem was the total unfamiliarity of the

instrument layout. On the mastery of this depended the speed of their departure in Addis. Twenty times over the next two days, both men fought to reduce the time of their take-off without ruining the engine.

Their instructor, Piet Osterhuis, was at first less than a perfect teacher. Collins had not told him the purpose of the training. The realization that he could not complete his job to his satisfaction and the feeling that information was being kept from him exasperated him. Only after the following conversation, on the afternoon of the first day, did his mood improve.

'I have no eye-dee, no eye-dee at all what you want to do this for. To take off in two minutes, one minute, I don't know? It matters so much? You have men chasing you with machine-guns?'

Collins, strapped into the pilot's seat, set a finger and thumb against the bridge of his nose in a gesture of exhaustion and suffering patience. He glanced round at Rourke in the seat behind, then with sudden decision leant across to the trainer and muttered conspiratorially: 'Yes. We are from British Military Intelligence. Please do not ask us more. We are depending on your training to save our lives.'

The change wrought by this piece of melodrama was instantaneous. From then on, Osterhuis used every minute to good effect, until, with much reduced checks, both Collins and Rourke were sure of being able to take off in less than a minute.

Saturday, 10 April
Yufru had already arrived at the bank, impeccable as usual, with his slim briefcase, which he at once opened. He slipped four sheets of paper – the visas – on to Cromer's desk and

accepted an orange juice, while Cromer poured himself his usual whisky.

Cromer had his glass raised in a toast to continued success when the phone rang. It was the weekend porter announcing Cromer's guests.

Within two minutes, Collins, Rourke and Halloran, all dapper in dark suits, with briefcases stamped with the Cromer seal, stepped out of the lift.

'Ah, Jeremy,' said Cromer. 'Mr Sackville-Jones, Mr Smithson, allow me to introduce Mr Yufru.'

'Indeed, gentlemen, a pleasure,' said Yufru, shaking hands with each in turn. 'Mr Squires, good to see you again.'

Then, as Cromer offered drinks, Yufru went on: 'I will not detain you. I have only a few things I wish to say. Firstly, I owe a debt of thanks to you all, and in particular to you, Sir Charles. You gentlemen are certainly very lucky in your employer.'

The three smiled and nodded.

'And the next thing is to reassure you about your visit. You will be honoured guests of our government at the Addis Ababa Hilton. A car and interpreter will be placed at your disposal. But there will be no official functions to attend. My government do not wish to emphasize your presence. Finally, it remains for me to wish you good luck. Perhaps we may meet again when your mission is accomplished.'

Collins, Rourke and Halloran had not said a word. Yufru, wrapped up in the significance of the occasion, merely shook hands with them all again and left. Cromer accompanied him downstairs. When he returned, he found his three colleagues relaxed and laughing in sudden relief.

'Holy Mother,' said Halloran. 'I may look like a banker but I feel a fucking idiot!'

'Pete, you are a fucking idiot,' said Rourke. 'A suit is no disguise. The buggers will suss you right away.'

Halloran frowned. 'Really? Major?'

'Don't worry,' grinned Cromer. 'You look just fine. Any of you need a job when this is over, just give me a call.'

8

The afternoon flight to Addis Ababa, with its stops in Paris and Rome, was uneventful.

The plane touched down at the Ethiopian capital's Bole Airport, an unexceptional collection of glass and concrete, at 6.05. As the engines were still dying, a black Mercedes pulled away from the line of cars in the lee of the main building and swung round beneath the wing to the steps that were being trundled into position. An announcement asked all passengers to remain seated. As the 'No Smoking' sign went off, an air hostess began to show the passengers off the plane.

Collins led the other two down the steps to the sleek Mercedes waiting on the tarmac. A uniformed driver sat at the wheel. Standing nervously by the back door was a small, neat man, grey-suited in the international uniform of bureaucracy. His top lip was pulled back in a nervous smile that revealed a keyboard of glistening teeth. He stepped forward to shake Collins's hand in welcome.

'Asfud,' he said. Rourke felt his small, bony hand twitching with nervousness. Asfud shook hands with the other three members of the delegation, repeating his name at each

139

self-introduction, and adding: 'Interpreter. English, Amharic, French, Italian. London, Paris, New York, Rome.'

Rourke wondered how a man so apparently terrified of life could have acquired that width of experience, or having acquired it, why he should remain so terrified. Perhaps it was an indication of the gravity of this particular meeting.

The Englishmen sank back into the cavernous rear seats of the Mercedes. Asfud climbed into the passenger seat. The car purred away towards an exit in the wire fence surrounding the airport, its progress monitored by two Ethiopian policemen who stood ready to close the gate behind them.

Addis Ababa was an odd mixture of modern splendour and long-established squalor. It was founded by Selassie's uncle, the Emperor Menelik, in 1892. At that time Addis Ababa, which means 'New Flower', was merely the latest in a series of temporary encampments that had each served as the capital until the surrounding woods were exhausted and there was no more fuel for cooking. But Addis turned out to be different. Its setting is delightful. It lies at 8000 feet, amid mountains that grow daisies, lilies and orchids, and its climate is moderate. Menelik, unwilling to move again, planted fast-growing eucalyptus trees for fuel, and the place endured. Soon, the Emperor built himself a palace, a two-storey whitewashed house, the only brick building in Ethiopia at that time. Other permanent buildings followed: workshops, barracks, offices, a chapel, a den for the palace lions.

Since then, much of the medieval squalor had remained unchanged: drainage was still almost non-existent in the outskirts, and there were always more beggars per square mile than anywhere else on earth. But at least this city of 800,000 had acquired a veneer of modernity. Hotels, hospitals, office blocks, shops, the houses of the rich, and the spanking headquarters of the Organization of African Unity, stood within a short walk of earth-floor hovels and tin-roofed huts. Menelik's eucalyptus trees, with their blue-green leaves, were everywhere, offering cover to the jackals and occasional hyena that crept into the city at night. Fiat taxis tooted at likely fares, and women watched over wayside stalls of onions, garlic, pepper and other spices. Everywhere – especially since the 1974 famine – there were beggars: pathetic, mangy huddles of rag, bone and flesh.

Into this once Imperial capital swept the Mercedes. It was a mere ten-minute drive from the airport to the Hilton, a four-square, nine-storey, grey and brown box lying in a fifteen-acre site of rough grass and scattered eucalyptus trees, complete with pool, tennis court and a children's playground. An oasis of civilization in a garbage-heap of a city. There, they were handed keys by a smiling, tail-coated manager.

In exchange, Rourke noted with some horror, they were asked to hand over their passports. This was standard procedure, explained the smiling manager, for unfortunately Addis still had its thieves. The passports would be kept in the hotel's safety-deposit box until their departure.

Their rooms were on the fourth floor, in line down the corridor. There was a distant view over the outskirts towards the towering western highlands that, along with the deserts to the north and east, have helped preserve Ethiopia's independence from lasting conquest.

Asfud informed the men, before they went into their rooms to unpack, that they were guests of the Ethiopian government and would not be required to pay for anything during their one-day stay, and requested them to enjoy the facilities of the hotel and to sleep well in preparation for the conference the next day. He would, he said, return with their car at ten the following morning.

For the next few hours, during which time the men retired to their rooms, showered and dined, scarcely a word was spoken. They agreed there was nothing to be done about the passports. A protest would merely invite suspicion. Otherwise, they were a little army before battle, each man alone with his own thoughts.

Sunday, 11 April

But for the lurid colours of the décor, they might have been in any international hotel anywhere. Without needing to be reminded, all three of them ate well and drank a gallon. There was no knowing when they would eat and drink again.

Halloran in particular was remote, his usual flow of superficial banter dammed up behind slightly lowered eyelids. He seemed drugged, robot-like.

At 10.12, the car awaited them.

There were no more words. Each man took his briefcase. In silence, they took the lift down to the lobby, where Asfud hovered uncertainly, and walked out with him to the Mercedes standing in the forecourt.

The Swiss Embassy was a ten-minute drive from the centre, to the north-east, one of the more graceful and spacious areas on the edge of the city, within a mile of the American, Russian, British and German embassies. There was no single diplomatic sector in Addis, though some embassies – mostly African ones – were grouped together near the centre. Like almost all except the smallest and most central embassies, the Swiss Embassy stood behind a fifteen-foot compound wall, topped with barbed wire. It consisted of one main, two-storey building and three smaller ones: a gatekeeper's lodge, a second small bungalow that acted as a guest-house, and a triple garage.

The Mercedes was unremarked in the town. The inhabitants were used to attendant hordes of OAU officials in chauffeur-driven limousines. The Mercedes stopped briefly outside the embassy's double iron gates, allowing time for the gatekeeper to identify car and driver, and then swept grandly through. In the recess of the forecourt, on their right stood another, smaller Mercedes – the Ambassador's – the Swiss chauffeur dozing in the driver's seat.

Two wide steps led up from the paved forecourt beneath a pseudo-classical portico: the building was constructed to a Swiss design when Switzerland first established relations with Ethiopia in 1926. On the steps stood a tall, dignified man of perhaps fifty-five: the Ambassador, formally dressed in dark suit, white shirt and grey tie. He looked the career diplomat *par excellence*: tanned, steel-grey hair, half-glasses. He was alone. The car stopped. Asfud came round to open the door for Collins, who stepped out on to the tarmac, already warm beneath a clear sky. The Ambassador advanced and shook him by the hand, then said, with the merest hint of an accent: 'Morges, Georg Morges. Won't you come with me?'

He led the way up the steps, stopped briefly until the other three were ready to follow on, then continued through an entrance hall, with stairs sweeping up to the first floor, and turned right, through ornate double doors with fluted, gold-coloured knobs and with bolts top and bottom, into what was clearly his own office, airy, spacious and lit by two casement windows. Both were closed; the embassy was air-conditioned. On a sideboard stood an assortment of drinks: juices, cola, tonic water, an ice bucket. There was no alcohol – out of deference, the Ambassador explained, to the Imperial dislike of it. There was also coffee on an electric heater.

The office, normally furnished with an ambassadorial desk, a low table and armchairs, was dominated now by a large conference table surrounded by eight solid, leather-covered

SAS Operation

armchairs, three along each side and one at each end. Each
place was laid with a pad, several pens and glasses of water.

Morges was cool. At his age, and with his experience, he
disliked having to hand over his embassy. It would have been
interesting, and more fitting, to have been asked to chair the
meeting, about which he had been fully briefed. But Zurich
had been adamant.

'I believe you will find the arrangements to your approval.
You will see that I have placed your delegation along that
side. The Emperor should sit at the head of the table. The
senior member of the Provisional Military Administrative
Council will be seated at the other end. The three other
Ethiopian delegates are along this side. This is as you requested.
It is as well to have matters properly arranged for such delicate
meetings.' The Ambassador allowed himself a brief, cold smile.
'Now, here is the anteroom . . .'

He walked to a second set of doors and swung them open
to reveal another, similar office – normally his own conference
room – more comfortably furnished with chairs and sofas.

'If either side should need private discussions . . . Now,
perhaps you will wish to arrange your documents and take
refreshments. Your opposite numbers should arrive shortly.
Then the Emperor's helicopter. But my instructions are to
leave the embassy at your disposal. I shall return later when
the Emperor has left.'

Collins took on his role of leading delegate. 'Herr Morges,
everything seems excellent, excellent. We owe your country,
and you personally, a debt of thanks.'

Clearly that was all that was necessary. Morges nodded
formally, without smiling, said merely 'Gentlemen' and left
the building, walking round the side to his Mercedes, which
swept him out through the gates. The gatekeeper allowed

the gates to remain open. Their own Mercedes reversed round to take the spot vacated by the Ambassador's car.

An uncertain silence fell. The three Britons stared down at the table. Asfud was as nervous as a gazelle. He glanced from Collins to the others and then at the refreshments table.

'Ah, Mr Asfud, please help yourself,' said Collins. 'Gentlemen, shall we?'

Each man named a choice: coffee for Collins, Coca-Cola for the other two. In addition, each of them downed another two glasses of water.

Rourke noticed a movement. He nodded towards the court-yard, where a Daimler was gliding in through the open gates. It contained three Ethiopians who would (with Asfud) make up the full delegation of four. The leader was a minister, Tedema, and with him were two aides, middle-aged financial specialists who had made a detailed analysis of the memorandum of transfer in both English and Amharic. All three were dressed formally in European-style dark suits. The gates were rolled shut and the Daimler stopped by the steps. The three passengers got out and the car reversed back through ninety degrees to park beside the English delegation's Mercedes, leaving the forecourt clear again.

The three men came straight out of the glare of the sun and in through the door as Collins moved toward them from the conference room. Tedema extended his hand.

He was a tall, thin man and remarkably young, in his early thirties. He was clearly enjoying himself in the exercise of his authority, as well he might, believing himself about to supervise the official receipt of some $2000 million.

'Mr Squires. How good to meet you.' He held on to Collins's hand as he spoke, a gesture common to many African countries, but one that Westerners often take for overt homosexuality, to their own embarrassment. His accent was too much of a perfection. Sandhurst, perhaps? Oxford?

Collins said: 'Mr Tedema, I am delighted everything seems ready. My own staff . . .' – he introduced each in turn, then went on: 'We have just established the seating plan as arranged from London.' He explained the arrangements, with the Ethiopian nodding rapidly.

'Good, good,' Tedema said. 'Let us be seated.'

Briefcases were placed on the table, documents removed from them and chairs pulled back.

At that moment, as they were sitting down, there came the distant sound of a helicopter. It was half a mile away and coming in low, with the deep thud of twin-bladed rotors. In seconds, the helicopter was over the parking lot, twenty feet up, above the spot where their Mercedes had first stopped half an hour before. Dust scudded away to either side, fogging the window. Collins walked away, back to the door, and through to the lobby. The others followed.

He waited until he heard the engine cut out and the rotors begin to slow. Then he opened the door warily and stepped out into the dying breeze. The helicopter stood some forty feet away. Its rotors swished to a standstill.

Through the reflections on the glass panels Rourke could see a man – no, two – at the controls, freeing themselves from their belts. The one on the far side opened the door, jumped down and ran towards the main gates. He was an officer and was wearing light army fatigues with a sleeveless jacket over a short-sleeved khaki shirt. He carried a light 9mm Uzi machine-pistol and a walkie-talkie.

Halfway to the gates, he stopped and signalled to the two chauffeurs with his weapon. The drivers left their cars and walked rapidly across the tarmac. The three men then hurried over to the gate. The officer waved his weapon urgently at the gatekeeper, who let them through, then followed, pulling the gates to behind him. The officer signalled the three civilians out of sight behind the wall and took up a position immediately outside the gates, at their very centre. Rourke was disconcerted to see one of the drivers emerge from the gatehouse with a rifle of some kind.

The nearside door of the helicopter opened to reveal the second pilot, also in officer's uniform. He stepped down, then turned, opened the rear door and unfolded some steps.

Collins had scarcely noticed the slight figure sitting behind the pilots' seats, in the centre of the aircraft. Through the glass of the door, he had seemed a mere shadow.

Now the shadow moved. It was indeed the Emperor.

The hook-nose and beard were silhouetted against the window beyond. He was in a seat placed in the middle of the rear section, which had been stripped of other seats for the purpose. The figure rose slowly, stooping and slight, and came to the steps. The officer, staring upwards, shielding his eyes from the noonday sun, held up a hand. The old man reached out and stepped down, three steps in all, to the tarmac. The officer moved back, in obvious deference.

The Emperor stood for a moment, his hand free again, staring down, as if in thought, or waiting for his eyes to adapt to the glare.

The officer took a couple of paces back to the helicopter, reached in and took out a walkie-talkie. He spoke into it briefly, looking up towards his colleague at the gate. Number two waved. Yes, the radio link was working fine.

Rourke's gaze focused again on the Emperor. There was no hint of grandeur in his dress. He wore a black cloak tied at the neck, over a grey jacket done up Mao-fashion and matching

147

trousers. His shoes were plain black leather. In stature, too, the figure was merely that of a very old man, shrunken, emaciated, five foot two in height perhaps, no more. He was a wraith, the spirit of a former age.

Yet almost at once his bearing clothed him in regality. Fifty years of near-absolute rule were too ingrained for easy eradication. His hair and beard, wiry and grizzled, framed a bony little patrician face. The eyes, penetrating and compelling, rose. The shoulders came back and the old man walked forward. Collins had read that Ethiopians had once prostrated themselves at the mere passing of Selassie's green Rolls-Royce. Now he understood why. The old man radiated an authority that was almost tangible.

'No protocol,' said Tedema, as if sensing Selassie's impact on the foreigners. 'He is nothing now.'

The Emperor, flanked by the second pilot, whose machine-pistol remained in the helicopter, slowly mounted the two steps. The party of British and Ethiopians fell back to either side to allow his passage.

With the officer solicitously at his side, Selassie proceeded into the hallway and turned through the open doors into the conference room. As the two entered, Collins moved alongside the Emperor and indicated the place at the head of the table. Without even glancing round the room, Selassie stood at the table head. The officer moved his chair out. The Emperor stepped into position, his chair was lifted in, and he sat, his hands on the arms of the chair, impassive, staring down the table while the others moved round to their own positions.

Asfud had reached the limits of nervousness, his eyes darting from Collins, to Tedema, to the Emperor, and then as if to retreat from the tension these sights loaded upon him, to the swirls of plaster decoration round the top of the walls.

The Emperor suddenly leaned sideways to Asfud as the final chair scraped its way into position. He said something in Amharic, so quietly no one else could hear. Asfud dropped his gaze in a gesture of submission and thanks, and from that moment on seemed calmer, strengthened by an infusion of imperial sympathy.

With everyone in their places, the officer, who had been standing behind the Emperor's chair, placed the walkie-talkie on the table by Tedema and indicated the on-off switch. Tedema nodded. The officer flicked the switch to demonstrate. The device emitted a little beep and a light flashed briefly on and off. Again Tedema nodded. The officer walked rapidly out without a word, leaving the room in silence.

Through the window Rourke saw him reach into the helicopter, lift out his weapon and walk towards the gates. He turned round to look out of the other window. The man slipped through the gate to join his colleague, to form a discreet guard outside the embassy.

Rourke ran a check. Weapons outside the gate: one Uzi, one rifle of unknown make, maybe a pistol or two. Weapons to hand: nil. Opposition: four inside, four outside, with a radio link. Outlook: dodgy.

Tedema, meanwhile, had begun a speech. Asfud was leaning forward to translate into the Emperor's ear.

'. . . as quickly as we can. I am here on behalf of the Provisional Military Administrative Council to sign with you and with the former Emperor the document before us. It is an historic moment for us. There must be no error. I suggest, therefore, that you read your English version clause by clause. I shall read the Amharic version. We shall then sign both versions. There should be no disparity. The translation has been checked already. The reading may take an hour, an hour and a half. But we shall all have confidence in the memo-randum at the end. Is that agreeable?'

The Emperor nodded. Rourke and Halloran were merely watchful.

Collins cleared his throat and began to read, pausing at the end of each clause so that Tedema could follow on with the relevant section in Amharic.

He read on until he came to the clause relating to the release of various grandchildren still under house arrest. This was the moment Collins had chosen to start the real business of the meeting. He paused, coughed, and looked round.

'Minister, Your Highness, I believe there is a further consid-eration to be, ah, considered in that preceding clause. It relates to the mechanism of payment to the members of the royal family abroad. I would like a brief recess to speak with, er, with my staff first, and then with the Emperor.'

Tedema stared.

The Emperor, his eyes closed in concentration, listened intently to Asfud's murmured translation.

'I think,' responded Tedema coldly, 'that we have done quite enough for the family. We owe them nothing. Yet they are to lead the lives of relatively wealthy people. I fail to see your point.'

'Let me explain,' said Collins. 'The family are to receive fifteen per cent of the total share. I should imagine that there might be some justifiable concern that the family's funds might be spent in areas that would not be wholly, how shall we say, to your country's interests?'

For five seconds Tedema made no response. Then he nodded slowly.

'Ah: subversion,' he said.

'Exactly. It seems to me that it might be possible to spread the payments over a longer period.'

Silence.

'A good point.' Tedema nodded again. 'Your obvious self-interest might after all work to our mutual advantage.'

All this while, Rourke had been merely watchful, waiting for Collins to give the sign for action. Now the moment had come, his senses suddenly focused. He had never been so close to action without a weapon, never been dependent on a colleague. He felt naked. What if they saw through him? Reached for the walkie-talkie? Ran for the door, shouted for the guards?

'Very well.' Tedema's words sent a surge of adrenalin through Rourke. 'You wish to recess? I think we can accept that.'

While Asfud muttered in the Emperor's ear, Collins deliberately pushed back his chair and selected a few of his papers. 'Shall we?' he suggested, with a casual smile to Halloran and Rourke. They both nodded, and followed him into the anteroom. Collins eased the door closed behind them, and moved away, across the room.

'OK,' he said, in a voice hardly more than a whisper. 'We let them be for a few minutes.' He glanced at his watch, then looked around, as if seeking inspiration from the room. Through one window, the two parked cars were half visible. To the left, stood the guest-house, shuttered and silent. The other window gave out on to nothing but the compound wall.

Collins nodded briefly towards the other door, which led out into the entrance hall. 'Do we have an alternative exit?'

'Not if they've got any sense,' said Rourke. With three swift strides, he was at the door, gingerly pressing down the handle. Then with a shake of his head, he returned. 'Rock-solid.'

They stood in silence. Halloran carefully undid a button of his shirt, reached inside, and pulled out his thin strand of rope. He wrapped it round his hands, then moved into position behind the door.

Collins looked at his watch again. 'Two minutes. Let's give them another one.'

'I hope you know your lines,' Rourke muttered. The idea of relying on words at a time like this unnerved him. He was glad Collins had the job.

'Act One is fine,' said Collins with a taut smile. 'It's the finale I need help with.'

He looked at his watch again, stepped forward and opened the doors, concealing Halloran. Collins coughed deferentially. 'We have a suggestion, Mr Tedema,' he said. 'But before proposing the matter formally we need to go through the wording with Mr Asfud. Mr Asfud, would you be so kind?'

With a nod from Tedema, the little man walked with his usual smile towards the ante-room. Collins backed away, leading him on. As Asfud came through the doors, Rourke closed them, leaving Tedema standing, smiling, his back towards Halloran, who stepped silently foward, the rope taut between his hands.

Asfud, who had clearly been expecting an invitation to sit down, opened his mouth and drew breath to speak. At that moment, Halloran's rope came round his throat, and, as if in a cold fury, the Irishman snapped his arms into a cross behind his head. The rope bit into the Ethiopian's skin. In silence, his eyes bulging, his mouth open, his hands scrabbling at his constricted throat, he sank towards death, as surely as on a gallows, suspended from Halloran's bent arms.

Even before the body relaxed, Halloran used the noose to haul his victim behind the door, where he laid him out. Asfud's feet drummed a soft, brief salvo on the floor, and a stain spread down his trousers.

'Good one, Peter,' breathed Rourke. Outwardly, he was calm, but it was the first time he had seen murder done in quite so cold a manner. He was at once hypnotized by the drama of death and exhilarated that it had been accomplished in such silence.

Halloran, still locking the noose around Asfud's neck, glanced round, assessing how visible the body would be when the next victim entered. He rolled up his eyes and grimaced as if to apologize for his own foolishness, and then dragged the corpse behind the sofa. At last, he seemed satisfied. He removed the noose, nodded at Collins, gave a small smile to Rourke and resumed his position behind the door.

'OK,' Collins said. 'Next.'

He adjusted his face to form an urbane smile, opened the door, and stepped across the threshold. 'Mr Tedema,' he said, with no trace of nervousness in his voice. 'Mr Asfud has no real problem with the language.' He glanced behind him, to one side, as if meeting Asfud's eye. 'We would like your comments before we place the changes before the Emperor.'

Tedema sighed. 'Will this take long?'

'Oh, no. A minute or two.'

For a moment, Rourke thought Tedema was going to object, because he muttered something in Amharic to his colleague and then to the Emperor. 'Very well,' Tedema said, turning to Collins. 'I suppose I had better come.'

The operation was as straightforward as the previous one. The door closed, and Tedema had time only to look around puzzled and begin a question: 'Where is . . .?' when the rope was round his throat, and he, a taller man than Asfud, was on his knees quivering in Halloran's iron grip.

For another minute, the four men formed a silent, fixed tableau, the only motion being from Tedema's fluttering hands. Rourke watched, intrigued by the sight of an intelligent,

153

supercilious, self-confident individual turning into a useless bundle of flesh and bone at Halloran's feet.

'Now what?' Halloran asked, as he dragged Tedema's corpse over to lie beside Asfud. He slid the noose clear, and slipped it into a jacket pocket.

'Two down, two to go,' Collins said.

Rourke was surprised to hear his own voice. 'We can't pull the same trick again.'

'What?' said Collins, already on his way to the door.

'Too risky. If they suspect . . . if one of them shouts out . . . if the last one switches on the walkie-talkie . . . the guards at the gate can see into that room.'

Collins paused and turned. 'You're right, Michael.' He spoke with his usual ice-cool tone. 'Not the same trick. We have to do this bit all at once. It's three against three. Peter and I will deal with the other two. Michael, you take the Emperor.'

'But the guards can see.'

'Only if they're looking. We have to move together, get into position behind each of them, then in unison get them against the wall, out of sight.'

All three waited, playing the scene in their minds. None of them doubted their ability to kill. The Emperor himself was a rag doll, easy to lift.

'Remember,' said Collins as if reading Rourke's mind. 'Treat the old man carefully. No use us arriving back with damaged goods.'

'Tell me again,' said Rourke. 'We rescue the young ones and kill the old one, right? Or is it the other way around?'

Collins shot him a wry smile, and glanced again at his watch.

There was only one question: could they preserve the element of surprise? Again, it was Rourke who put it into words. 'Who does what exactly?'

'Let's get on with it, for Christ's sake.' Halloran's voice was a whisper, but it rasped with urgency.

'Wait.' Collins's expression was calm. 'We can afford the time. We're still bankers. We've been talking business in here. When we go in, they'll be expecting the other two to be right behind us. We'll have maybe five, ten seconds' grace before one of them flips. In that time, we have to be behind each of them without arousing suspicion. I know . . .'

He moved to the table and picked up the papers.

'We've all been studying these, OK?' He broke open the binding on the cover, and divided the bundle into three. 'One for each of them,' he said.

Halloran opened his eyes wide. 'What's it supposed to be?'

'Draft revisions. In longhand.' Collins caught the sceptical gazes of the other two. 'I know it's dumb. But it's good enough to get us into position. Any better ideas?'

Silence. Rourke shrugged.

'OK. Back in character. Let's go.'

Collins stepped forward, depressed the ornate door handle, and opened the door. Rourke saw him smile broadly, ready to greet the two Ethiopians at the table.

'Mr Tedema . . .' he began firmly, then broke off.

The two remaining Ethiopian officials were not at the table. The Emperor sat, with his back to the doorway, as before. But the two aides were at the window, smoking, staring out towards the main gates. And one was holding the walkie-talkie. Clearly, he had just been using it. Rourke could see straight over their shoulders. There were the two pilots, backed by the two chauffeurs, standing idly, in full view, staring towards the Embassy. One of them raised a hand in acknowledgement, and the aide did the same, his cigarette languidly resting between his fingers.

He turned, and graced Collins with a grin. 'Wonderful toys they have nowadays,' he said.

Collins's smile froze. After the briefest of pauses, he said in the same bold voice: 'Gentlemen, we have a solution. If you would take your places?'

Rourke and Halloran moved into position behind Collins, both seeing instantly that if either of the two men showed a hint of suspicion, if there was any danger of waving at the guards or calling for help through the walkie-talkie, they would have to move together, fast.

The man with the walkie-talkie stood smiling, waiting. He glanced at the room behind Collins.

Collins turned and addressed the empty room. 'Mr Asfud, Mr Tedema, thank you. We are waiting.' He turned back to the aides. 'They are finishing the translation. Meanwhile we have the original. Allow me.'

And he moved decisively towards the table, extending his papers ready to put them down for the aide. Halloran was right behind him, making for the man's seat. Rourke moved into position behind the Emperor.

'Ah, yes. Of course.' The aide slowly placed the cigarette between his lips, and switched off the walkie-talkie. He walked to the table, placed the radio on it, and sat down. He picked up the papers.

The other aide had moved across the room and just sat down, with Collins behind him when a puzzled expression crossed the first man's face.

'I don't understand. What is it you wish me to read?'

Halloran stood back a foot, and reached into his jacket pocket, feeling for his rope as if for a pen.

'Oh,' said Collins. 'How foolish. The wrong page. Please turn over.'

The aide did so. Halloran's hand came unnoticed out of his pocket.

There was no need for any word.

Collins raised his arm, turned sideways into position, and brought the edge of his hand down in a vicious backhand chop into the neck of the man in front of him. He would have felt nothing. His head snapped backwards. Even if the nerves running down his spinal column remained intact, the shock was enough to snuff out consciousness for hours. He slumped forward, clouting his nose on the table, probably breaking it, releasing a stream of blood.

At the same time, Halloran garrotted the other aide. This, of course, was certain, but it took longer, and proved noisier than the previous two murders. The man's knees came up sharply beneath the table, and his body jerked the chair about as if it were electrified.

All this occurred far more quickly than it takes to tell. And meanwhile Rourke's task was to secure the prize, the Emperor himself. Rourke had been so absorbed by what the other two were about to do that he had given no thought to what it would feel like to grab the old man.

Silence was the first requirement. Restraint next. Those two alone would have been easy: a hand over the face, an arm round the shoulders. But there was no point in silencing and pinioning Selassie, only to find he had the Emperor trapped in his high-backed chair. Before making a move, he had to be aware of longer-term needs: mobility and safety.

The answer was automatic. Even as the first man crashed on to the table and the second began to fling himself back and forth to escape Halloran's noose, Rourke slipped his hands over the chair back and under Selassie's arms, scooping him up as if he had been no more than a tailor's dummy.

157

As he lifted the Emperor, he thrust his left hand clear and clamped a hand over the old man's mouth.

Swinging him away from the chair, and back against the wall out of sight of the guards on the gate, he held his burden firmly clear of the floor. He was light, no more than 100lb. And he had no time to do more than utter a few muted grunts. But he was not quite the rag doll Rourke had been expecting. There was still a surprising amount of strength in the wiry little arms and shoulders.

The sight before the Emperor was, of course, something of a stimulus. The two government men before him were dead or dying. The two others had vanished. True, they were enemies, and in other circumstances he would have had them executed anyway. But right now, there was no telling what the mad Englishmen would do next. All he knew was that they were killers. For all he could tell, he was next. So he panicked, and struggled, his tiny feet kicking out at Rourke's shins, his arms flailing.

Rourke was suddenly at a loss. Their lives depended on getting clear, quickly, with Selassie. That meant subduing Selassie. But not hurting him. Keeping the Emperor's head held tight against his own chest, Rourke changed grips, locking his free arm right around the Emperor's body and both his arms.

'Keep still!' muttered Rourke in the old man's ear. 'We've come to save you!'

Collins was watching Halloran, who still held the aide round the neck. The man was almost dead, but Halloran was not yet ready to let him go. At Rourke's words, Collins looked up, to see Selassie twitching in Rourke's arms.

'Wiry little bugger,' said Rourke. 'I don't know what to do with him.'

Collins put up his hands in a gesture of appeasement, and spoke directly to the Emperor.'

'Listen, sir, Your Majesty.'

Selassie swung his head from side to side in a vain effort to escape from Rourke's iron grip. His eyes were wide, and breath wheezed through his nostrils. He made muffled little noises – 'mm . . . mm' – behind Rourke's hand.

'Christ, listen! We are here to rescue you! Just do as you are told and everything will be all right!'

Something seemed to get through. Selassie stared at him, and the struggling ceased. Rourke relaxed his grip as much as he dared.

'OK,' said Collins. 'That's better. Listen: we have been sent by Sir Charles Cromer. We are not bankers, we are soldiers. He wants to rescue you. We are going to put you in that helicopter, and get you out of the country. Then you will be safe. OK?'

Selassie stared, and did not struggle. Rourke gingerly relaxed further. Halloran had left his victim, and was standing watching, his right hand idly putting away his garrotte. Collins glanced round to make sure they were all out of sight of the guards.

'You understand?' said Collins. Still the Emperor stared.

'Let's move,' Halloran said impatiently.

'We need him,' Collins muttered. 'And we need him to go quietly.'

At that moment, a sound intruded. It was a small electronic beep. Instantly, all four were transfixed. On the table, beside the slack body of one of the aides, the walkie-talkie had come to life. Its little light glowed. A metallic voice came through, speaking in Amharic.

'Kill it!' Halloran said.

'Sh,' whispered Collins. 'The circuit's open.'

The voice ceased. Then it came again, more insistently.

Rourke whispered: 'They'll be wanting to speak to Tedema.'

Collins looked at Selassie. 'Speak to them,' he said, whispering tensely in Selassie's ear. 'Just tell them everything is OK.'

Selassie stared.

'We have to trust him,' said Collins. 'Let him go.'

Gingerly, as if he were handling an unexploded bomb, Rourke released the old man.

As Rourke's hand came free from Selassie's mouth, there was a few seconds' silence. Then the walkie-talkie squawked again.

Selassie yelled one word, a high-pitched shriek, struggled clear of Rourke's arm, and made for the door.

He had taken no more than two paces when all three of them reacted. Rourke and Halloran grabbed him, and then, just as he opened his mouth to shout something else, Collins brought a fist down on the scrawny neck. The old man collapsed on to Rourke's arm.

'Jesus, major. You said to be careful with him.'

'We're not going to get him out if he's shouting his mouth off. Hold him until we see what damage he's done.'

'What the fuck did he say?' asked Halloran.

'God knows,' muttered Collins. 'But it's time to go. With or without his co-operation. Look.'

Across the courtyard, the gate was swinging open. The pilot with the machine-pistol was coming to check up on what he and his mate had heard: a puzzling shout for help in Amharic.

'We could do with his weapon,' Rourke said.

Collins nodded, and signed Halloran to take up a position behind the main doors. Then he glanced at the offending walkie-talkie on the table, still with its light on. He walked over to it, leaned across the dead aide, and lifted the handset. He threw a switch. The light blinked off.

There was a shout from the gate. Halfway across the courtyard, the pilot stopped. His mate yelled something.

'They know something's up,' Collins said.

Seconds later the pilot had disappeared from sight, having reached the building.

Rourke caught Collins's eye, then glanced down at his burden. Collins nodded towards a spot on the floor to one side of the door. Gently, Rourke laid the unconscious Emperor on the floor. A thought flashed across his mind: strange creatures, humans – to be so careful with one individual, while preparing to use extreme violence against another.

They heard the main door open, then close again with a click.

Silence, broken, to the open-mouthed astonishment of Rourke and Halloran, by Collins remarking in a conversational tone: 'Well, I guess the silly bastard's waiting to see if we killed off his bosses.' He paused and glanced at Rourke. 'Am I crazy? Not yet. The sod with the gun the other side of this door is waiting to see what the hell is going on in here. And the one thing he'll be expecting to hear is someone talking. Well, I'm fulfilling his expectations for him, and I just hope he doesn't speak English.'

Rourke cleared his throat. 'Oh, yes, I quite agree, sir. Very steamy weather for the time of year.'

'That's it. Let's just keep talking then, while we make quite certain that our reception is ready. Mr Halloran, would you do the honours?'

The handle of the door went down. Halloran's hand already held the rope. The door opened a crack. Collins stepped across,

161

and pulled it open further, with a ready smile for the wary pilot, careful not to allow the man much of a view into the room, and then turned slightly as if addressing an unseen audience: 'I wonder if it's OK to allow our friend in here?' He nodded in feigned acknowledgement of an instruction, stood back, and beckoned.

As the pilot appeared round the door, Rourke just had time to see an expression of horror cross his face at the sight that met his eyes – two bodies at the table, the Emperor lying apparently dead on the floor – when Halloran's noose went round his neck. The gun fell, swinging by its shoulder band. The pilot's hands locked on to the rope, his fingers seeking a hold. He was strong, this one, and he had had some training. Finding no finger-hold to release the garrotte, he brought his bent arms sharply back to elbow Halloran in the ribs. The Irishman kept his grip.

Rourke and Collins had expected this death to be as silent and as easy as before. This time, though, the pilot was more than a match for Halloran. His neck was still brutally constricted, but now his legs kicked backwards, and his body began to thrash, not in a death throe, but in retaliation.

'Rourke!' Collins's voice snapped him back to conscious thought. 'His arms!'

It took the three of them to complete the death, with Collins and Rourke gripping the pilot's arms, and forcing him to his knees, while Halloran, grim-faced and sweating, wrung life from the weakening body.

When it was over, they stood back and surveyed the mess of the conference room.

'You be nursemaid,' said Collins to Rourke. 'We'll back you.'

While Collins detached the gun from the dead pilot, and Halloran went through the man's pockets, Rourke again lifted the delicate body of the Emperor. He paused briefly to feel the pulse. Yes, there it was. He looked up at Collins. 'OK, sir. He's a bundle of bones, but he's alive.'

'Let's get the hell out.'

Halloran had found only a pocket knife. Muttering in disgust, he stood up and checked the window.

The gate was closed. The guards – the second pilot and the two chauffeurs – were watching the Embassy curiously. The driver with the rifle was standing with his weapon at the ready.

'And two pistols,' said Halloran. 'At that distance, not a problem.'

Collins ran a rapid check on the pilot's gun. 'It's a Williams carbine,' he said. 'Haven't handled one of these in years.' The semi-automatic rifle had a full magazine. He flicked off the safety-catch and settled the weapon into the crook of his arm. 'Peter, go for the chopper. Check if there's a weapon in there. Michael, you follow him. Sling the old man in, and strap him in. We don't want him recovering consciousness and trying to throw himself out. I'll get their heads down, and then start her up. That'll be our weakest moment. Peter, if you haven't found anything else, you'll have to take over this thing' – he slapped the carbine – 'until take-off.'

The two men nodded.

'OK. Go!'

Halloran ducked through the door, leaving it wide for Rourke. At the main door, Halloran opened it, allowing Collins to speed past him. Collins ran into the middle of the courtyard, sank to one knee and fired at the gate.

Behind him the two men ran for the Bell. Rourke caught a glimpse of the three men at the gate, with spurts of dust flying around their feet. One was flat on the ground – dead? – another beginning to force the gate open, and the third beginning to aim his rifle. Clearly they weren't ordinary chauffeurs and pilots, but trained soldiers, able to respond even when taken by surprise.

Then Rourke was at the chopper. Halloran was already inside.

'Shit!' No weapon, but there was a box of ammunition. He whipped out a magazine, turned, hauled Rourke up the steps with his spare hand, and jumped down to take over from Collins. Rourke was concentrating on dumping the unconscious Emperor into a seat, and then dragging safety straps around the frail old man. Even as he clicked them closed, he was dimly aware of more bursts of fire from Collins, and another noise: incoming fire, cracking into the chopper.

Through the noise, Halloran yelled: 'The major's hit! Michael! Get started!'

Rourke looked out. Collins was down, a bullet in the knee. He was dragging himself towards the helicopter, while Halloran jumped out and, crouching low, seized the weapon and fired a burst at the gates. Most of a mag was gone, but it did the trick. There was no one to be seen: keeping their heads down.

The gun died, out of ammo.

A figure appeared round the gate's side column, aimed a rifle and fired.

The spare magazine was on the ground beside Halloran, who squatted and snapped off the old magazine.

'Goddam it!' Collins, hit again. The shoulder this time. He rolled over, and began an agonized, snake-like wriggle towards the helicopter.

Meanwhile Halloran had smacked the new magazine into place, aimed and fired. Bullets puffed off concrete, zinged off metal, sent dust scudding up the road from around the gate.

Rourke was in the pilot's seat. How long had this been going on? Seemed like an eternity of slo-mo action, long enough for all of Addis to know there was trouble, long enough for the whole fucking army to mobilize . . .

Rourke addressed the controls. He threw switches.

Fuel boost.

Mixture.

Throttle.

Ignition.

No time for any other checks. No time for the seat belt.

The rotors began to swing above him, the whine of the turbines building, building, until it blotted out the noise of gunfire ten yards away.

Ahead, the gates were open now. Someone would be on a telephone, surely, asking for back-up. The body he had seen lying in the road was gone. So maybe they hadn't taken a casualty after all. So there were still three out there, with just Halloran holding them back.

And now Halloran's second magazine was empty. He turned, leapt into the helicopter, grabbed another mag, and then jumped out again to cover Collins's gasping progress. The wounded man was five yards from the chopper . . .

Halloran slapped in the new mag . . . four yards . . . Halloran aimed, fired . . . three.

The Bell's turbines had reached full, deafening power. Rourke stared down at Collins, unable to do anything for him. The down-draught tore at the major's hair. His banker's suit was a mess of torn material and blood. He mouthed words through the noise and his own pain. Rourke shook his head, unable to read his lips. Behind him Halloran was still firing.

Rourke heard the rattle of Halloran's fire stop, saw the gun-smoke die. Halloran glanced down at Collins, hesitated for a second, then decided. He tossed the weapon into the helicopter's open door, stooped, got an arm under Collins, jerked him to his feet. Collins was sinking now, his eyes beginning to roll, blood loss and pain sapping his consciousness.

The chopper was ready. Halloran yelled something into the major's ear. It was useless. The older man sank beneath him. Halloran went down too, supporting him.

At that moment, Collins jerked. Rourke looked up. The bastard with the rifle was at the gate. A cool one, that – to fire accurately at a time like this. Now he had hit Collins a third time.

Rourke saw him aim again, at Rourke himself this time, the deliberate, controlled action of a professional, and fire. It all happened too fast for him to react. A little hole appeared like magic in the windshield, prettily framed in a filigree of shattered Perspex. It seemed to Rourke he could see straight through it, and clean up the barrel of the marksman's rifle. How the bullet had missed him, he couldn't understand. He felt wet on his hand, saw blood. He was hit. But he hadn't felt the impact. No pain. He felt his shoulder, then his face, followed the trail of blood with his hand. His *ear*, his right ear was bleeding. Even then, with the helicopter trembling to be gone and the turbines whining and the wind roaring, Rourke thought: Jesus, that guy is good.

He looked down again. Halloran was dragging Collins towards the door. He tried to lift the wounded man. In films, it looks easy. In real life, to lift an unconscious man is almost impossible. It's not the weight. It's the distribution of the weight. There's no way to get at the centre of gravity or keep the burden rigid, as Halloran well knew. For a few seconds, he wrestled uselessly, then he turned, and waved an arm violently at Rourke: Take her up!

Rourke pushed the control lever. Above him, the angle of the blades changed, biting into the air, hauling the machine into the air. He glanced behind him, in time to see Halloran leap on to the skid just as it left the ground, and grip the surround of the open door for support. Beneath him lay Collins's body – it had to be the body, for the last shot had caught the major in the side of the head.

But which way? Not up. Away, to the right, as quickly as possible out of range. He turned the stick, too hard. The machine swung round and tilted, no longer gaining height. Ahead was the compound wall, fifteen feet high. He wasn't going to make it. He righted the machine, it clawed for height: ten feet, twelve . . .

At that moment, Rourke looked back to check that Halloran was safe. What he saw plunged him into further horror.

As the chopper righted itself, Halloran lost his grip, screamed, fell backwards, then, as if by a miracle, seized hold of the skid. For a second he hung there. He was still hanging when the helicopter cleared the wall, no more than a foot or two above the barbed wire. The wire tore him off the skid like a fly hitting a spider's web.

Rourke hoped he died instantly.

He swung his gaze back to what lay below and ahead: roads, houses, the suburbs of Addis.

Rourke risked one more glance behind. The embassy was receding. He could see it all now, the main building, the garage, the gatekeeper's house, the two parked cars, Collins's body in the middle of the courtyard, and the marksman standing beside it, pointing at the receding helicopter. He didn't fire. There was no point now. The machine, with its strange burden, was already out of range.

9

Rourke, his once immaculate suit covered with dust, hugged the contours. The lower he flew, the fewer people would be able to see him, and the better chance he had. Not for long, of course: Ethiopian Air Force planes would soon be out looking for him. No need to make it easy for them.

Sweat seeped down from his armpits, soaking his business shirt. He grabbed his tie – fuck's sake, a *tie*, in these circumstances! – and yanked it off.

Where to for the best?

Less than 200 miles south lay the first stop on his escape route: Lake Chamo, with its hidden store of fuel. But wait one. What if Collins and Halloran were still alive? He wondered briefly if there was any chance they would divulge the escape route, then dismissed the thought.

Below him unfolded the outer fringes of Addis, a few brick houses, wood-and-tin shanties, a decaying factory or two, then only scrub, rocky outcrops and a dusty road. He glanced at the compass. He was heading north.

He could afford to hold course for another minute. Anything to sow a little confusion in the opposition. Air speed: 110 m.p.h. Fuel: almost full – 300 miles' worth, give or take.

Rourke felt the adrenalin begin to leave him. He took a swig from the flask of water dangling from the instrument panel, and wondered if there was any possible alternative to heading south.

There was none. He had no idea of the country, except what he had seen on the map. North: Eritrea – a breakaway province who would no doubt love to get their hands on the Emperor, if only for propaganda purposes. But too far. He wouldn't get halfway. East: desert. West: mountains. That was it.

Besides, it wasn't just himself he had to consider. He stole a glance at the Emperor, still unconscious in the seat behind.

OK. Half a minute more, and he would make his move. He planned his course of action: to head back the way he had come, but further west along the cliffs and folds that scarred the highlands, hoping they would hide him from the radars and eyes of anyone on the lookout for him.

He checked his fuel again – and stared in horror. The gauge had dropped sharply. Now, suddenly, after flying for – what? no more than five minutes – it read three-quarters full. Even as he watched it, the needle edged down a point.

How the hell could this be happening? At once he knew the answer: the marksman.

There had been other shots, not all of them at the three men. At least one of them had come at him. He touched his ear. It was caked with blood. Nothing serious: a nick. Some blood, no pain. Perhaps the shot hadn't been for him at all. That was why it had missed. Perhaps the man had been aiming at the fuel tank, or a fuel line. Or perhaps there had been other shots Rourke hadn't been aware of, a ricochet. Whatever, the fuel was leaking away.

Instantly, he reassessed his situation. He couldn't make his fuel dump on Lake Chamo. If he tried, he might not even get much beyond the populated highlands. If he was spotted, he would just be a sitting duck. He'd be caught, probably killed, the Emperor recaptured and killed, the whole enterprise in tatters.

There had to be another way.

North, after all, to Eritrea? It was too far by hundreds of miles for him to fly the distance, but – his mind spun a fantasy – perhaps land near a road, hijack a vehicle – he had the carbine Halloran had thrown in the back – and then maybe he would be able to smuggle Selassie into hiding, find a telephone, call London, fix up funds, get them to send a plane. After all, he had possession of one of the most valuable political prizes in the world. Surely, they – the government – the Foreign Office – Cromer – *someone* – would want to see the two of them safely out.

Too much wishful thinking, he decided. Start again. He was heading north-east, to avoid populated areas. Go with that. What was in this direction, east? He remembered the maps he'd seen in Collins's house, in Chris Swain's office, in the plane flying north to make his fuel dumps. Yes, the Horn of Africa: Djibouti.

If he remembered right, Djibouti – the border anyway – was only about 300 miles from Addis. Now that was a more realistic possibility. They spoke French there, didn't they? Once over the border, he would be able to improvise something through diplomatic channels. He would keep the SAS's name out of it, but after all, he had Selassie.

Selassie was the key. He would be coming round shortly, and Rourke had to have him on his side. Surely to God he knew some English, enough for Rourke to explain what was happening, enough maybe to get some help from the old man. Once he understood he owed the Britons his life, surely he would be happy to help.

171

'Hey!' he shouted above the whine and throb of the engine. 'Sir! Your Highness!'

Still looking ahead, he found he could reach back far enough to shake the figure behind him. Selassie seemed to have slumped forward in his harness. His head lolled. Rourke felt for his shoulder, and gave him a shove.

Then he looked back. An arm fell clear. It swung and juddered in time with the beat of the rotors.

He reached a second time, and pushed the old man's head. It fell back. The eyes were open.

A new, different panic gripped him. The vacant eyes, the limpness, face slack, chest unmoving . . . The Emperor was not unconscious. He was dead.

Flying time: half an hour, and falling.

Rourke's face creased in an agony of frustration. Below him the shadow of the helicopter chased over grey, dusty soil, scrub and thorn bushes.

The true ghastliness of his situation hit him. He had been contracted to save the Emperor from a murderous regime. Instead, the mission, even in its success, had accomplished precisely the opposite. Moreover, Selassie's fortune had not been saved for the West. Now it would be locked away in perpetuity, and the sole beneficiary would the fucking bankers who had got him into this mess in the first place. To cap it all, a successful escape had now taken him from the frying-pan into the fire – literally, by the looks of the landscape below.

Flying time: fifteen minutes.

A herd of gazelle scampered off to one side below him. In the distance he saw a vehicle, spewing dust behind it as it bumped along.

'Shit!'

The one thing he had to ensure now was invisibility. Hah! He gave a bitter laugh. Him – invisible! He was dressed in a grey suit flying over a wilderness where they spoke Christ knows what and spent their time castrating foreigners, piloting a damaged chopper where there was no other plane for hundreds of miles, running out of fuel, about to land in a furnace of a place, without water, and – if he did come across someone who might offer help to such a surreal creature – to cap it all he was carrying the one man whose face would be instantly recognizable to absolutely the entire population.

The body. His mind focused on the only thing he could do to improve his chances. He had to get rid of the body.

He veered away from hills on his left, out over desert.

The 'fuel low' warning light flicked on.

Do it now!

Rourke pulled back on the stick and slowed his progress over the desert. He checked the horizons, liquid in the heat. No sign of human life. The only movement was a gliding bird, a vulture probably, riding the thermal from some baking rock over a mile away. He dropped down, aiming for a gravel patch near a few low thorn bushes.

The skids touched the sand, the rotors whirled to a stand-still, the dust of the landing scudded away and settled. Rourke opened the pilot's door and climbed out. The heat smote him, rising up as if from an open oven. He looked at his watch: 2 p.m. At least the sun was sinking. It could only get cooler from now on.

Standing on the desert floor, he at last removed his crumpled and stained jacket. There was no relief. But at least the heat would dry the sweat from his shirt.

He turned to the rear door, still locked open, and reached for the straps holding the tiny corpse. The skin was wrinkled

173

like stained parchment. Nothing in this sack of a body to indicate imperial greatness. He clicked the belt open, and the body slowly keeled sideways, on to Rourke's outstretched left arm. He brought his right arm up, took the Emperor round the chest and slid him out, on to the ground. He left him lying on his face, laid the cloak along his back, and weighted the edge of the cloak with pebbles to stop it blowing about.

He stood back, and checked. There was nothing but a scattering of thorn bushes, some sparse palms a few hundred yards away, and off to the west, the trembling ghost-images of mountains emerging from the haze.

For a second, he considered covering the whole body with stones, but he had been out of the chopper for five minutes already, and every second meant less fuel and more danger. What was the point in building a grave? It would turn a temporary thing – the vultures would do their work in a few days – into something lasting, which might eventually draw attention.

He climbed swiftly back into the Bell, and punched the starter button. Ten minutes of flying time left – twenty miles at most. He wondered briefly if he had made the right decision. Perhaps after all he should head west, towards the hills, find a road and transport . . .

No. People meant danger. He would have hundreds of miles to go in hostile territory. Better trust to his survival instincts in the desert and get over the nearest border.

The dust roared away from his rotors, covering the little corpse, but also dragging the cloak free of the pebbles and setting it flapping madly. The helicopter rose, the ground vanished briefly in a haze of blowing dust. When it cleared, the chopper was thirty feet up, and as Rourke tilted away eastward, he saw that the body was nothing but an insignificant smear.

Keeping low, he flew on, over nothing but the same featureless flow of dust, rock and scrub. Nothing here to make him choose one place over another. He recalled the forbidding notes on the Operational Navigational Chart: 'limits of available vegetation information' . . . 'insufficient data for contour lines' . . .

Any towns? None that he could recall. But wait: that phrase on the chart – 'numerous camp-sites and sheepfolds' – gave him hope. If there were people, there would be food, water, clothing, and perhaps some means of transport: donkeys, horses, camels, something.

Something somewhere, perhaps, but not here, not in this hell-hole, not in time. If he didn't land right now, he would end up in a heap of wreckage. As he pulled the stick up, bringing the chopper to a shuddering hover, he saw, fifty yards ahead, a track, hardly more than an absence of scrub and rock, but enough to outline a course used for some human purpose: going somewhere, driving animals.

It was enough. Fuck it, he had no choice.

He drifted off to one side and came down in a shallow defile, probably a watercourse – if it ever rained. He sat there for a moment after the whap-whap of the rotors died away and the turbine ceased its whine, feeling the heat and the silence. He was below the level of the track, invisible unless someone came to the lip of the defile. He could afford a minute or two to gather his thoughts.

The water-canister swung idly from the instrument panel. He drained it, and wanted more. In this heat you had to have those eight pints a day just to keep going, and he didn't give much for his chances of topping up over the next few hours.

He climbed out to piss – there went another valuable pint – then retrieved first the carbine, then a clip of ammunition from the case, and finally his jacket from the floor. He sat down in the shade of the chopper and checked the weapon. He had handled a Williams carbine in training, when they had to try out every foreign weapon the SAS could get their hands on.

He knew the story: Williams was a moonshiner doing time in a US prison – this was in the 1940s – and to pass the time he designed a new gun action in his head. It was an original conception, allowing for a very short, quick and reliable return. Later, he actually started to make the damn thing in the prison workshop. The authorities slapped him down, of course, but someone had spotted what he was up to, and acquired the patent. Colt put the gun into production, and soon there were four million of them arming the US forces. They lasted through until the A3 16 replaced it in the early 1970s, at which point the Williams carbines were unloaded on to the open market, some of them filtering through to Third World countries.

Rourke reloaded, then folded the jacket into a pillow and lay down on it to plan his next step.

He took stock.

Business suit, one, banking executive, for the use of.

Hand-made leather shoes: one pair.

Tie: one. Particularly useful, that. A chap should always have a nice striped silk tie when stranded in the desert with a downed helicopter.

Water: nil.

Food: nil. But come to think of it, he didn't mind, yet. Christ, was it only that morning he had breakfasted so lavishly in the Hilton? His mind told him that it was centuries ago, in some other universe. His stomach told him otherwise. That was something to be grateful for.

Fuel: nil.

Prospects: terrible.

Sense of humour: very, very low.

There were, however, a couple of pluses. Weapons: one. Ammo: as much as he could carry.

Sometime, someone would come looking for him from the skies. If they sent a plane within two miles of his landing-site, the Bell would stand out like a prick in a nunnery. He wondered whether he should try to camouflage or destroy it. Camouflage? With the amount of vegetation round there? Forget it. Burn the thing out? And release a smoke signal that would bring the Ethiopian cavalry over the hill? Besides, burn it with what?

Sod it. Just get out. If he stayed here, he would simply dehydrate and be dead in two days.

Except it was still mid-afternoon, and the sun was hammering down, and it was just plain daft to move during the day. He knew the rules. This had to be 120 in the shade. He guessed he had a litre's worth of liquid in him. If he moved at night and lay up in shade during the day, he might survive through the next day, and ought to be able to walk about twenty-five miles, max. So unless he wanted to commit suicide, or he heard a plane, he would stay right where he was until nightfall.

His mind played with memories of desert survival training. Watch birds: circling birds might indicate the presence of water. Camels shit near wells, so if you see mounds of camel shit, watch out for a dried-up water-hole and get ready to dig . . . A voice sounded in his head, some officer who had come to lecture them on the delights of the American barrel-cactus . . . must look out for cactuses . . . cactuses . . .

* * *

177

He woke with a jump.

It was dark, and wonderfully cool. The Bell loomed over him, a shadow against a starry sky. A glow low in the sky told him there was a moon. He blinked, lay still, looked and listened. Something had woken him. Behind him – he could see it clearly outlined as he twisted round on an elbow – was the dark line that marked the edge of his little world. He might have been alone in the universe.

But he wasn't. He heard a shuffling sound, and a sort of panting from close by, above him. He rose quickly, grabbed his jacket and weapon, and ducked down the other side of the helicopter.

Over the edge of the defile a head appeared.

It was a goat, nibbling at a low thorn bush.

Rourke watched. In his experience, animals seldom went off too far on their own. Where there was one goat, there could be others, and where there was a herd, there would be a herdsman.

The goat retreated. There was no further sound.

Rourke waited, straining his ears, waiting for his eyes to gain full night vision. If there was anyone nearby, there was no hint of movement. He needed information. Slowly, he stepped around the chopper, then walked carefully up the gentle fifty-foot slope of the little valley. A crescent moon, low in the sky, came into view, dimly lighting the desert landscape.

There was the goat, browsing by itself a dozen yards away. Odd that it was on its own.

Then he saw a pinpoint of light, flickering – a fire – perhaps a hundred, two hundred yards away. Hard to tell the distance in those conditions.

He sat down again, and thought through his options. He needed food, water and clothing. If there was any walking to do, it would be good to have something comfortable to walk in – these thin-soled shoes would give him hell after a few miles. The camp-site might offer all these things.

If he could get them without revealing himself, so much the better. Of course, he could go in gun blazing, take out however many people were there, and go on his way. But he could not bring himself to regard an Ethiopian peasant as his enemy. Anyway, discretion would serve him better. God knows how far the sound of gunfire would carry on still desert air, and it wouldn't take an Ethiopian Sherlock Holmes to draw conclusions from a pile of corpses and an abandoned helicopter.

He put on his jacket – it was getting cooler by the minute, and if this little op took more than a couple of hours he would need warmth. Besides, it provided a way to carry extra ammunition, just as a precaution. He walked gingerly back down to the Bell, reached into the box of clips, and slipped two of them into the two inside breast pockets – enough for some security if he didn't make it back to the chopper. Finally, he retrieved his empty water bottle.

He set out towards the distant glow, picking his way between the moonlit bushes. His leather soles scrunched noisily on the desert floor, but there was nothing but the goat within earshot. Still, in response to his training, he stopped every ten paces to listen.

Then, in the middle distance, perhaps 150 yards away, there was a figure, small and stooping: the herdsman. Rourke squatted down, and watched. The man seemed to be casting about. Looking for his bloody goat, probably. Anyway, he had – Rourke hoped – left his camp-site unguarded. The herdsman was moving away from him. Rourke walked as rapidly as he dared towards the fire.

As he approached he saw that the camp was closer than he thought. The fire, which was burning low, had clearly been used for cooking. Moreover, it was not just a chance camp. The moon glinted off the tin roof of a shack, from the other side of which, Rourke could now see, a fence ran, forming an animal pen. Against this darker shadow, the fire glowed. He stopped again to listen, and could now hear the soft rustle of moving animals. More goats.

Then a sickening groan. Rourke grimaced. To anyone who had never heard it, the noise would have sounded like a soul in torment. Rourke, though, knew the sound of old: it was a camel, over by the fire by the sound of it.

He hated camels. The most disgusting sight he had ever seen was an Arab slobbering in tears over a camel caught in the belly by a 66mm anti-tank rocket. It was hard to know which he found the most revolting: the camel's wounds or the beast's slimy green death-spittle.

The place seemed deserted. As a precaution, Rourke removed his shoes, inserted them into the side-pockets of his jacket, and padded in his socks – fucking socks! in the desert! – slowly up to the wall of the shack. There was a door, made of loose wattle. He stood for perhaps five minutes listening. Nothing, not even a snore. The herdsman out in the desert behind him must be alone.

He gave the door a push with the barrel of his weapon. It opened.

Inside was a table, hardly visible in the faint glow of moonlight that came through the small, unglazed window and the half-open door. On the table were a variety of objects: the remains of a meal, Rourke discovered, when he placed his water bottle down and explored with his free hand. His gentle touch revealed a few pieces of fatty meat and some *injera*, chapatti-like unleavened bread, hard, gritty and bitter, but perfectly edible.

Rourke was chewing when he heard slight noises from outside, a foot kicking a stone, a cough, a nose being cleared. He moved against the wall behind the door, deeper into the shadows, pulling his dark jacket well across his shirt, and folding the lapel up over his face. He heard the noise of a piece of fence being moved, a slap, a protest from a goat – the same one, no doubt, that he had seen earlier, now retrieved by its owner.

What now? Rourke already had two possible scenarios. The first involved the herdsman settling down by his fire, leaving Rourke to finish his meal, collect whatever might be useful from inside the hut, and be on his way.

The second scenario had the herdsman entering the hut. So when the door swung open, Rourke was ready.

A figure entered, dressed baggily in a *shamma*, the toga-like shawl that is part of the national dress of Ethiopia. He was a middle-aged man, Rourke guessed. He walked straight across the room, mumbling to himself, picked a large leather water-container out of the shadows – good to know that was there – took a long draught, and replaced the container.

He turned. Perhaps he caught a glimpse of Rourke's bottle on the table. But he had no time to react, for at that moment the side of Rourke's fist caught him just below the right ear. He went down like a marionette with its strings cut. It had been a delicate hit. Rourke checked the herdsman's breathing and pulse to make sure he was still alive.

It took perhaps two minutes for Rourke to strip off the man's sandals, baggy cotton trousers and *shamma*. He changed out of his own clothes, carefully setting on the table his two ammunition clips and the machine-pistol, then bundled the clothes together for later burial: no point in leaving more clues than necessary. He dressed in the loose peasant clothing, discovering to his amusement that the trousers were held up by a belt made of elastic braces.

Then, prowling the hut, he finished the rest of the bread and drained a brackish litre from the leather flagon. Most of the rest he used to fill his own bottle.

'Thanks, mate,' he said, to the unconscious man naked on the floor, taking up his bundle in one hand and his weapon in the other. The clips he inserted into the improvised waist-band of his trousers, and left.

Outside, he looked around at the moonlit desert. What now? And where? He could head east by the stars – there, low on the horizon, was the Plough, its two right-hand stars pointing at Polaris, true north. But he had no idea how far the border was. Two days' walk? Or two weeks'?

There was no getting away from it: the sensible thing was to use the effing camel. He went over to it. Beside it was a blanket and a saddle. Another blanket lay on the ground. The camel was couched, reins in place, looking at him with disdain.

'I don't like this any more than you,' Rourke muttered.

He tossed the blanket and saddle over the camel's hump, forced the saddle strap through behind its front legs, and tightened it. He climbed aboard. With a dreadful lurch, the beast rose. He shook the reins, and was off.

With luck, the man would assume he had been robbed by a *shifta*, or bandit, and simply not bother to report the loss. He would be on his way in the morning, probably with his remaining blanket as clothing. By the time Addis traced the chopper and arrived here, the herdsman would be far away. At worst, he would see the helicopter, and make a report. By then Rourke would be long gone.

10

Monday, 12 April

Eight hours later, Rourke was twenty-five miles further east, and the worse for it. The only time he had broken his journey was to scrabble a shallow hole to bury the suit and shoes. If there was a trick to riding a camel he had never cracked it. In Oman, he could never relax into the trancelike state achieved by his Arab squaddies. Now, as the hidden sun began to threaten the eastern horizon, he was sore with the chafing of the saddle at the base of his spine and the pommel between his thighs, and horribly tired. The early exhilaration – the sense of freedom, the cool of the night, the hard glitter of the stars, the monochrome expanse of the empty desert (he had seen not a living thing all night) – all that had evaporated after a couple of hours. That was when the aches had started, and his mind had begun to dwell on the imme-diate past.

He had lost a colleague and a mate. He relived the pain he had seen written on Collins's face, saw again Halloran's doomed attempt to save his boss. Dicky wasn't always a bundle of laughs, and Peter had his faults, but when it came to it, they had fought well together. Quite like the old days for a few minutes. Could he have done more? He replayed the murders in the embassy, the ridiculous attempt to win Selassie's support, Collins's well-intentioned but fatal blow.

No, he couldn't see too much to reproach himself for. They had walked the knife-edge that always divided success from failure, and luck – as often in warfare – had pushed them off the wrong side. Now it was up to him to survive, to make some sense of deaths that would otherwise be meaningless. He – and the story – had to be their memorial. Who dares wins. For Rourke, as for every SAS man, that remained the guiding principle.

But, for the present, just to survive he had to find a place to lie up through the day. The camel seemed in fine fettle after eight hours, but he had no way of knowing how long it would go if he tried to ride through the day. Camels were odd creatures. Once, in Oman, he and his men had come across an oasis where two of the beasts lay in the shade, motionless. His guide explained they were dying. They had become fatally exhausted. They had been made to travel too far, too fast, without enough food, until their legs started to give way. Eventually, their owners would have been unable to make them rise, and had simply left them to die, too weak to eat or drink yet surrounded by food and water. Perhaps another day of walking would reduce this creature to a useless lump. He was surprised to find he cared. The animal had carried him for eight hours, lugubrious but uncomplaining. If he was ever human in some previous incarnation, he was surely a butler.

More to the point, though, he himself would not survive the day. He was already in need of water. Two hours in the full sunlight would turn him into biltong.

He looked around in the strengthening light. He became aware of how very obvious he would be if anyone happened to see him, a lone figure in the middle of a gently rolling plain of sand, rock and gravel. Herdsmen might accost him, brigands assault him, a military helicopter or light plane swoop down to question him, if not spot him immediately for what he was.

He urged the camel up a rise, and cast about for anything that might offer shade. To the west, the desert lay in deep purple shadow; to the east, the dim light already made the ground grey. Off to the south-east, another ridge attracted him. Perhaps a ridge would lead to a dip, and a dip might offer – what? A rock shelter? A tree?

'Come on, Jeeves.'

He slapped the reins and the camel swayed forward. It moaned as it broke into a stiff-legged run, forcing Rourke to lean back to keep his balance. The edge of the sun appeared almost ahead, bathing the desert in a golden light and casting vast long shadows from tiny contours and shrunken thorn bushes. For the first time, as the camel slowed at the bottom of the ridge, Rourke was struck by the beauty of the wilderness around him.

He came to the next ridge, climbed it and looked down. It didn't look promising. It was perhaps twenty feet deep. The only steep slope faced the rising sun, and would shortly turn into a suntrap. The bottom still lay in shadow, and seemed to offer nothing except a single scrawny bush.

He scanned the horizon again, and was now surprised to see something which must have been there all along, but now stood out sharply: mountains, their angular peaks spotlit by the sun. Suddenly, he knew where he was. These were the mountains that funnelled down into the Rift Valley. If he could only follow them, they would lead him south-west, and then south, and take him directly to the only other spot he knew in this stricken land: Lake Chamo, where he had been only a few days before, laying up fuel for the escape.

Well, that was then. The world was different now. Even if he could have covered those 200 miles, it would be of no use. He was better off with Jeeves, a half-empty water bottle and a thorn bush.

He urged the camel down the slope to the bush, where the creature nibbled at a branch.

'Hey, that's my house,' said Rourke, hauling Jeeves's head up.

The bush was only waist-high, and had no leaves. It would offer no shelter from the heat. But there was a foot of space between the gravel floor and its lowest branches. Rourke saw that he would be able to use it as a support for his blanket.

He dismounted, carefully and painfully, then took off the saddle and blanket, leaving Jeeves standing. He spread one end of the blanket across the bush, and was gratified to find that the thorns hooked neatly into the material. The other end he held to the ground, fixing it firmly with rocks, gravel and sand. He had a makeshift but effective tent, in the best traditions of the SAS.

The very thought of lying down and sleeping seemed to sap the last of his energy. He took a long draught from the bottle, leaving a pint of the warm liquid to refresh him when he awoke, and prepared for sleep.

But what to do with Jeeves? He would need the camel that night, but he didn't like the idea of him standing about all day right over the little camp. He led Jeeves 100 yards along the defile, pulled the reins down and tied them to two rocks. It wasn't much, but there was no time now to come up with a better solution. Jeeves collapsed on to his knees, and started rumbling, bringing up some ancient meal to re-chew. If he was like the camels Rourke knew in Oman, he would keep this up for several hours, and happily rest there until nightfall.

Then Rourke walked back, his feet in shadow, his head already feeling the heat of the rising sun, to his shelter, put the carbine down on his jacket in case of trouble, took the two spare magazines from beneath his belt, shuffled himself carefully under the low, sloping blanket, and slept.

When he woke, the light was dying. His only memory of the day was a succulent dream of Lucy, welcoming him to her, she offering her breasts. Then things had become very mixed up, because she had been talking to an old man, who was both Selassie and his father, and he had told the figure to go away, but the figure had pointed a gun at him, and he had woken to the sun shooting little rays through the material of the blanket above him. He reached out a hand and touched a rock. It was still burning. The blanket had done its job well, protecting him from direct light, allowing him to sleep right through the heat of the day.

As the sun went down and the shadows lengthened across the floor of the defile, he allowed himself a few minutes of luxury to plan his next step. He was almost out of water. By dawn he would be thirsty. He had no food. Another eight hours, and he would be hungry too. But he couldn't suppress a feeling of confidence. As the chart had indicated, there really were 'camp-sites and sheep-folds' scattered across the wilderness. Sometime over the next few hours he would come across a track, and the track would lead on eastwards, and he would find a source of food and water.

As he dragged himself out from under his blanket, and walked up the defile towards the shadowy far end of the defile, where Jeeves was waiting for him, he was already wondering about the border, already planning his arrival at the British consulate in Djibouti, already improvising an

187

unlikely dialogue with a tall public-school chap wearing a Guards tie who lived in a white-painted house complete with flag-pole, and always observed the Queen's birthday . . .

Except that the camel had gone.

He swung round. No sign. He ran up the slope, stared into the deepening twilight, even yelled 'Jeeves!' then shut up, for his voice would carry half a mile in the still air. He cast about, looking for tracks, and found them after ten minutes. They led away westwards. He presumed camels had a good sense of direction, and Jeeves would have known the area. He was off back to his master, or to a well, leaving Rourke quietly muttering 'Fuck' over and over again as he came to terms with the magnitude of his loss.

After cursing himself for his complacency – he must have been closer to collapse than he knew the previous night to have left the camel out there like that – his training took over, and he became coldly rational.

It was at least night. He could walk without immediate fear of dehydration. He would be able to cover ten, maybe twenty, miles. The hills he had seen were over *there* – he oriented himself by the glow of the setting sun – so if he headed due east, he would eventually find a track, a camp-site, a herd, a well, *something*. All he had to carry was his blanket, bottle and gun.

Really, he told himself, it was not much worse than Test Week during SAS Selection. If he could carry a heavy bergen thirty-five miles up and down the Brecon Beacons, he could make twenty miles on the level. If he could come through a bit of 'beasting' – like watching a truck drive away from an RV just as he arrived after a ten-mile run fully laden – he certainly had no need to let an AWOL camel get to him.

It was dark, and the cooling air was sucking the heat from the desert floor. He gathered his gear, and started walking.

When walking, running or marching, by far the most important item of equipment is footwear. A blister is not as bad as the runs – and God knew what that goatherd's bread was made of or what sort of camel filth had been swimming in his water supply – but it can be the death of you. A blister grows, spreads, bursts, making every step agony, wasting time, sapping energy.

Within five minutes Rourke knew he was in for it. The herdsman's sandals were mere strips of leather bound up with material. There was no way they could protect Rourke's soft feet. He felt raw spots developing on each side and where the material chafed his uppers. It was inviting pain, and perhaps infection, to wear them at all.

Now he was barefoot, picking his way across sharp rocks and gravel and desiccated twigs of thorn bushes as carefully as if he were negotiating a bed of nails. His progress was slowed from the punishing 4 m.p.h. he had planned to a meagre one or two. He was, in effect, a cripple, and after eight hours of skinning his soles on this barbed-wire surface, he would be one in fact.

He stopped, and held his head in his hands, creasing his eyes in anguish.

'Fuck!' he yelled, hoping now that someone was there in the void. 'Fuck! Fuck! Fuck!'

Even as he bellowed his frustration, he knew what lay ahead. The options were few. He would stagger on, in hope. If he found help, he survived. If he didn't find help, he had eight hours of hobbling misery followed by a slow and agonizing death from thirst. He could hole up for another day, but eventually, sometime in the next forty-eight hours, the desert would claim him. He knew because he'd seen it: the raging thirst, the cracked lips, the hallucinations, the collapse, then death.

189

The one thing he would not do was sit and moan.

He stepped forward gingerly, and grimaced as he trod on a pebble. Some of the men used to keep their feet hard, just in case, by going barefoot for weeks at a time on leave. It took about six months to harden your feet, and even then you had to be young – younger than Rourke was.

He was about to step forward again when, on the still night air, a sound came to him. It was a distant rumble that he immediately assumed was thunder. That made no sense. The night was clear, and rain about as likely as a pregnant Pope. Besides, the noise was continuous: a steady . . . not so much a rumble now as a . . .

It was in fact a perfectly ordinary sound, one he had heard so often he had instantly dismissed it as an impossibility. Then, once he had identified it, he became fearful that the extraordinary experiences of the last two days had flipped his mind. He waited, half expecting the sound simply to vanish, and leave him with the fearful certainty that he was hallucinating.

Now came confirmation: a low, distant whistle.

It was a train.

He stood, incredulous. No doubt now. The slow clack-clack of wheels across old-fashioned links, the steady roar of a diesel engine.

Suddenly, he knew it *had* to be a train. He saw again the map at their first briefing session. So much had happened since, he had wiped it from his memory. When they had been considering the best way out, they had thought about going east. Collins had pointed out the desert, the border, the impossibility of setting up dumps there, and the railway, heading down from the highlands, out eastwards along the northern wall of the Rift – the mountains he had seen the previous evening – and then north to the border, and Djibouti.

The noise was beginning to die.

'Hey!' he shouted, and began hobbling like a lunatic towards the sound, grimacing and grunting at each pace, at each sharp pebble that etched itself into his tortured feet.

Then, blessedly, it was sand and smooth rock. He sprinted, then stopped to check his direction. There came the noise – the distant rumble, the soft, seductive toot – further away now. He ran again, ran until the breath tearing in and out of his lungs drowned out all other noise.

His right foot hit something – a root? Even as he fell, he was aware of the damage to his toe. His arms flew out as he fell, with agonizing force, on to something extremely hard. His shins and forearms were skinned, his ribs assaulted as if by a metal bar.

He lay, writhing, splayed across metal and wood.

He had found the railway line.

'Oh, Christ,' he moaned, rolling over, sitting up, eyes shut in pain, winded, not knowing which part of his body to tend first: feet, arms, legs or ribs.

Gradually, his universe opened out. Shock and pain gave way to concern. He was sitting up in the middle of the track. To either side, the rails ran off into darkness, glinting in the light of the stars and a crescent moon hanging low in the sky. If he hadn't been in such a hurry, he would have seen the damn thing from twenty yards away. Idiot. Another mistake.

The train, of course, was gone.

A number of thoughts careered through Rourke's mind. How often did trains run along this Godforsaken line? One a day? A week? A month? No: the track looked in good nick. It was shiny, the result of regular use. But this was not exactly Clapham Junction. It was a single track. That meant the trains had passing places, widely scattered. The trains had hundreds of miles to travel. If they had to wait for each other, the timing could only be approximate. It was hard to imagine how they could arrange for more than about one a day.

And he had just missed it.

He looked longingly down the track.

Another thought penetrated the fog of laboured breathing and pain. He had been running towards the track, with the mountains ahead of him, and the train had vanished to his right, towards the highlands, towards Addis. He was staring west, not east. For his purposes, it had been going the wrong way. That meant, perhaps, there would be another one coming the other way.

Soon? Or in twenty-four hours?

One thing was certain: when it came, if it came, he had to get aboard it.

He took stock. He was standing barefoot in a stony desert, dressed in a filthy robe, carrying a blanket, a gun and an empty water bottle. That was all. Survival training hadn't prepared him for anything quite so basic. In survival exercises, you usually have something going for you – matches, a mirror, a Swiss Army knife, a candle, a razor – that can lever some advantage from your surroundings.

His only tool was his gun, and that was no help in survival. He had already been in two minds about carrying the thing with him at all. When you're weak, every extra ounce is a burden. But he knew he had to keep it. He could use it to shoot an animal for food. In extreme circumstances, he would have shot Jeeves, torn him apart with his bare hands, and chewed his raw meat like a jackal. If it came to it, he would eat a vulture or a snake. And later perhaps, if he survived, if he got out of this mess, and found himself back among people, a weapon might come in very handy indeed.

He sat by the edge of the track, occasionally standing to experiment with his damaged body. There was nothing seriously amiss. Plans formed, dissipated, reformed. He wondered about using the gun to hold up the train. Too risky. There was no guarantee the driver would stop, and he would have advertised his presence to no effect.

Find a slope when the train might be travelling slower, and leap aboard? Wild West stuff was all very well in the movies, but the train would have to be travelling very slowly, not much more than 10 m.p.h.

Stop it, then. He could have done with Jeeves. Stand him over the track, shoot him, block the train with a dead camel. Or with rocks.

What if the train was guarded? Ethiopia was falling apart. Anything of value, even passengers, might warrant protection. Anything odd, like an obstacle on the line, would be bound to arouse suspicion. He saw himself hobbling out from behind a thorn bush to board the stationary train, only to be confronted by a dozen soldiers.

Now he was beginning to formulate the problem in real terms. How to slow, or stop, the train without arousing suspicion?

He squatted, grabbed the blanket, knelt on it, and explored the tracks with his hands. There was no rail-bed. The sleepers were laid right on the desert floor. The track was narrow, he noticed, several inches narrower than the standard gauge back home. He felt the rails. They were still hot from the day.

Heat.

A fire.

Wooden sleepers! Set fire to a sleeper! Surely a driver would slow as he approached a fire, if only to ensure that the train could proceed safely. Perhaps from a distance it wouldn't arouse all that much suspicion – curiosity maybe, caution, but fires were natural: a bit of glass, a spark would do it.

So he would see it and slow down. But how far away would the fire be seen from? Rourke glanced down the line. At night, a fire would show up for miles.

A thought struck him. The last train had been travelling at night. Perhaps the trains *only* travelled at night. During the day, the carriages would turn into ovens and it would be hard to keep ancient diesel engines cool. Why risk turning a relatively easy journey across a flat and featureless landscape into a death-trap, with a broken-down engine and passengers dying of heat stroke? Wouldn't engineers, passengers and railway officials all agree that this should be a night-time service?

If so, he had no time to waste. The train had, say, 150 miles of desert to cover during the night. It would putter along at – what? 20-30 m.p.h.? That sounded about right for an African train running along a narrow-gauge track without firm foundations. So he was talking about a five-to eight-hour journey. It made sense.

Dawn was at six. It was now 11.06. Jesus! Get moving! But how? He had no matches, no lighter, no fuel.

Fuel wouldn't be a problem. There were enough thorn bushes around to make a fire, a small fire anyway, but he could hardly spend the night hauling armfuls of thorny twigs in from the desert. Besides, it would be tinder dry. Get the timing wrong, and the fire would burn out before the train ever got to it. OK. A small fire, to be lit when he heard the train.

And finally: ignition. The old boy scout stand-by – rubbing sticks together – was a non-starter. As a new recruit, he had seen fire made by hand, on his jungle survival course in Belize.

The Indian who did it had a softwood base into which he twirled a fire-stick to build friction, and eventually produce a spark. But both sticks were kept as carefully as matches, and they were far less convenient. The only purpose of the sticks was to teach survival techniques to people who would never use them. Even the Indian didn't need them. 'So that's the way you do it, at home?' Rourke had asked admiringly, through the Army interpreter. The old Indian had given him a withering look, and produced a disposable lighter from his shorts. 'You live like the ancestors if you wish,' he said. 'Not me.'

As Rourke stepped gingerly from bush to bush, breaking off twigs, he realized that he was carrying the only means of starting a fire: his ammunition and the Williams.

Contrary to popular belief, it is not possible to start a fire simply by firing a bullet into tinder. The bullet may be heated by the explosion and the friction of its passage down the barrel, but it never approaches the temperature needed to start a fire. You can even fire a bullet safely into petrol without risk of doing so.

Rourke knew what to do. His only problem was that he had never done it. And since he could only start the fire when the train was approaching, he would have just one chance.

With an armful of thorn bush twigs, he picked his way back to the track, to the blanket he left lying beside it, and piled the twigs over a sleeper.

Then he set to work on the first bullet. He placed it slant-wise between a sleeper and the rail, and pressed against it with his thumb. It gave slightly. He turned it, and pressed again. When the lead felt loose in its casing he pulled it out like an old tooth. Carefully, he tipped the powder into a little heap on the sleeper beneath his pile of twigs. Then he did the same thing to three more bullets. That gave him enough powder for a good flare, more than enough to make the twigs blaze up.

The last bullet would demand more careful handling. Once he had removed the lead, he put the cartridge down, making sure none of the powder tipped out. Then he teased a few strands of wool from his *shamma* and shredded them into a soft fluff. Choosing a couple of the thinnest twigs, he broke them and ground them into the palm of one hand with the heel of the other. The powdered wool and wood would be his tinder.

It was at this moment that he heard a sound. He paused, and listened. Silence.

Then he heard it again, and this time it did not fade away: the distant rumble of metal wheels.

With redoubled concentration, he transferred the tinder into the open-ended cartridge, then, as the rumble increased in volume, he blocked the end firmly with more strands of wool, and carefully replaced the cartridge in the breech of the rifle. He rammed the breech closed, and slipped off the safety-catch.

The principle of what he was planning was sound enough. He would place the muzzle against his little heap of gunpowder, then pull the trigger. When it exploded, the gunpowder in the cartridge would set the tinder alight as it travelled down the barrel. The speed and power of the explosion, unconstrained by the bullet, would dissipate quickly, emerging as a puff of smoke with hardly the force of a thunderflash, a grenade simulation. On leaving the barrel, the tinder would scatter into the gunpowder, and – if everything went right – blast it into flame. In theory.

In practice, the blast, small as it would be, might well simply puff the gunpowder away and scatter the twigs. Far from creating a fire, he might simply blow it to bits.

The train was perhaps half a mile away. At 20 m.p.h. that gave him one and a half minutes. He heard the rumble separate itself out into the clack-clack of wheels over rail joints, the clank of carriage-hooks, the throaty roar of a diesel engine.

To enclose the blast from the end of the barrel, Rourke needed a pad of some sort. He tore hard at the edge of the blanket. It did not give.

A minute.

He ripped at the *shamma*. Again, no good.

'A pad, a pad, a pad,' he muttered, and wiped sweat out of his eyes.

My hand, he thought, I could use my hand. But he pushed the idea away, not willing yet to risk a burn, or worse.

He tried the blanket again, heaving at it in a fury of frustration. It would not tear.

Half a minute.

There was only one thing for it.

He placed the muzzle of the gun on the sleeper, positioning it by feel against the heap of gunpowder. He inserted his right thumb into the trigger. His left hand he cupped over both the muzzle and the gunpowder, making a combustion chamber.

No time for further thought. If he thought any more, he might not do it.

He pulled the trigger.

There was a sharp crack, a flash from beneath his left hand, and then sudden, searing pain. Involuntarily he snatched his hand away and smacked it against his chest.

As he had hoped, it was all over so fast that the burning tinder had had no time to burn him badly. But his hand had been there long enough to do the job. The gunpowder had not scattered, and the tinder had fallen back into it. He watched in fascinated apprehension for the longest second of

197

his life. Then with a swoosh and a burst of fire, the gunpowder came to life.

He leaped up, still holding the gun, grabbed the blanket, and ran back some thirty yards over the desert, the sudden surge of adrenalin driving out any consciousness of painful feet.

Behind him, the mass of dry twigs blazed up, casting a lurid light across the surrounding desert. Rourke threw himself down, below the level of the scattered bushes. In daylight, he would have been easily visible. But he knew he would well hidden by the night, as long as he kept low enough to stop the moon picking up any of his contours.

The fire leaped and crackled, joined now by the sound of the approaching train. He couldn't see it yet, but it must be only 100 yards away. There was no way the driver could miss seeing the fire.

The sound came on, but with no screech of brakes or alteration of rhythm. And then there, a solid block of shadow, its green front flickering in the firelight, was the train itself, rocking on its narrow footing.

When it was a mere ten feet from the fire, there came a yell from the cab, the slam of metal on metal, the groan and shriek of brakes. It hit the fire with its wheels locked, scattering the twigs in a cascade of sparks, and sliding to a stop a few yards past Rourke's position.

In the dim moonlight, all was silent for a few seconds. He couldn't see yet – his eyes were still readjusting to the gloom – but clearly the driver had climbed down. He shouted something. Another man joined him. They appeared as two shadows out of the bulk of the train, walking back to examine the line.

Now Rourke could see more details of the train itself. It was a dinky little thing, with a diesel engine at the front, two freight-cars and a passenger carriage. He had imagined that perhaps it was like one of the old trains in Westerns, with a veranda stuck on the back, handy for grabbing hold of when you were running after it. No such luck. Doors all round, but no rear deck.

The two crewmen – shadows edged by moonlight – were now wandering about behind the train, kicking at rails and, Rourke imagined, the debris of the fire. The driver must have been half asleep. He could have had no clear idea what he had hit, or whether the line or his train was damaged. But it wouldn't take them long to find out.

One of the men shouted. Then a dishevelled figure emerged from the passenger carriage, with a small torch. Its small beam danced about along the carriage side, then down over the tracks towards the first two. All three squatted down. They had found Rourke's makeshift hearth.

Rourke wondered about sneaking up to the front of the train while the three had their attention on the ground. But there was no telling when they might stand, look around them and wonder who or what had made the fire, and if he was up and moving he would be only too clearly visible.

He could lie there, and hope they would simply wander off along the other side of the train. Possible, if they were checking it. On the other hand, they might split up, make separate circuits, in which case he would be in view of one of them all the time.

There was one old trick that might attract them away.

He felt around for a stone, checked the men – they were still squatting over the scorched sleeper, talking in low voices – stood, threw the stone as hard and as far as he could beyond the train, and ducked down again, flattening himself on the desert floor.

Rourke did not even hear the stone land. One of the men stood up. But his attention was still on the track. The conversation continued in a murmur of low voices.

Shit. Next time, the risk would be greater. He felt for a larger stone, keeping his eye on the men through the low filigree of branches. The one standing was half turned away.

Rourke rose to a squat, stood and hurled the stone with all his strength in a flat trajectory a few yards clear of the end of the train. This time, he heard it as it bounced once and scudded across gravel.

The men turned sharply. One said something, and walked towards the source of the noise. He vanished the other side of the train, leaving the other two watching.

Rourke waited in an agony of suspense. If the third man was going to return, best run now, best to risk the run with only two men visible. But if the other two joined the first man, then he would be able to reach the train with virtually no risk at all.

He took up the gun, stood, took a pace. Number two changed position. Rourke went to ground.

There came a shout from the other side of the train. Number two and three walked in that direction. Their shadows merged with that of the train.

Now!

In a flurry of sand and gravel and little sharp stones kicked up by his bare feet, Rourke, swerving round thorn bushes, covered the thirty yards in about ten seconds.

Then he was by the front of the train, squatting down, holding the gun across a knee clear of the ground, and gulping in air as slowly as possible, to suppress the noise of breathing.

He looked through the train's wheels. There, faintly, he could see three pairs of legs, and heard the murmur of talk. There was some minor disagreement going on, probably over the meaning of these strange events: first an inexplicable fire, now an inexplicable thump. One voice was assertive, another noncommittal, another wheedling – two officers perhaps discussing what was happening, against a driver worried about staying on time.

The legs moved towards the front of the train. Rourke moved along the track in the opposite direction, losing sight of the legs for a few seconds. He squatted down and looked through the wheels again. The three men were by the engine now, clearly coming right round the front of the train.

He reached up to try the door of a freight-car. It felt locked. He couldn't risk jerking it – it would make too much noise – and tiptoed on to the other one. Same thing. Christ, if they came round the corner now they would see him. No time to reach the last carriage.

He inserted himself in the gap between the second freight-car and the rear carriage. There were buffers. He ducked underneath, and squatted down again, with the buffers above one shoulder and the carriage-link – two heavy-duty hooks joined by a chain – above the other. He held the Williams vertically between his knees. The two spare magazines still firmly beneath his belt pressed painfully into his stomach.

Stupidly, he was facing the wrong way. He twisted his head, and forced it low. He had been just in time. Two pairs of legs were moving towards him. The driver had apparently climbed back into his cab. They would be moving off within the minute.

The two men went right by him. For a second as they went past, he could see them clearly picked out by moonlight. They were wearing military uniform. The one he could see most clearly was the worse for wear, with his jacket undone. He must have been rudely awakened by the shrieking brakes and sudden stop.

Rourke saw them stop at a door, heard them open it and get in. He looked up. Just above his head, above the chain-link connection between the cars, was a door. It gave on to a little platform that acted as a walkway between linked carriages. To reach the door, he would have to grab the platform, climb on the chain . . . No. Stupid. It would take him straight into the arms of the officers, and God knows who else inside.

From the engine came the whine of a starter motor, followed almost at once by the roar of the diesel. With a hiss and a clunk, the brakes disengaged.

The train was about to roll away above him, leaving him sitting once again in the middle of the track, in the middle of nowhere. He had to climb right now.

He stood in his narrow space, reached for the little walkway beneath the door to act as a handhold, and slung a leg over the chain – just as the engine engaged.

With a crash, the chain snapped taut beneath his thigh, lifting him clear of the ground, and nipping flesh agonizingly between two links. He yelped, and almost lost the carbine as he reached up with his right hand to seek another handhold. For a second, he hung as the links ground away at his trapped skin. Then the train lurched, and the chain bent again, enough to release him before it again took up the strain.

The train picked up speed. He worked himself into a safer perch, his feet dangling almost on to the sleepers flicking past below, his left hand still gripping the platform, his right hand holding the carbine.

Now, for the first time, he noticed, on the far side of the door above him, a slim ladder bolted on to the carriage. He could get on the roof. But it was not easy. He was astride the chain (though he didn't like the thought of what might happen if it bent and snapped taut again. Lucy would be left with precious little to keep her happy). It would have been easier if the gun had had a strap, if he had felt able just to push it aside and use two hands.

Eventually, in this confined, dark and shaking little area, he managed to fix one foot against the freight-car's hook, place the butt of the rifle on the platform, and lever himself into a standing position. Then he reached over, grabbed the ladder, swung a foot across, and was on his way up. He caught a glimpse inside the darkened carriage: wooden seats, slumped and sleeping bodies, bundles everywhere.

On the roof, the world seemed a distinctly better place. The train was moving at an easy 25 m.p.h. across the vast, open bowl of the moonlit desert. Away behind – he was now sitting facing backwards, enjoying the feel of the warm wind massaging his sweaty body – the track stretched in two glistening ribbons. In the far distance, he could even see the ghostly shape of the mountains, ragged against the low-lying stars. It was really quite beautiful.

The most beautiful thing of all was the sense of freedom. Not long before he had faced the prospect of covering no more than a couple of miles an hour, in pain, until he died of thirst. Now he was being carried in ease and comfort towards a sanctuary he should reach before dawn.

He lay down on his stomach, crosswise over the carbine, on the curve of the roof, savouring the moment.

11

It could not last. There were a couple of stops, which set him on edge. But it was still dark, the few buildings were all single-storey, and the two or three bleary passengers who got off could not have seen him.

Sometime, there would be the border. He played with the possibilities. Stay right where he was? Risky. It might be broad daylight, or there might be lights, or observation towers. Jump off – which was possible, if he chose the right patch – and sneak across the border, out of sight of the guard post? It didn't sound too bright: he would not know exactly when to make his exit, or how far it might be to civilization, and he would be hungry, thirsty, and barefoot. Still, it was an option. He peered ahead, into the wind, determined to see the border in good time.

As it happened, events decided matters for him. It was just before 4.30 a.m., and still dark, when the door below him swung open. He heard male laughter. He tensed, but could do nothing except keep the carbine hidden beneath his body and baggy *shamma*. A second later, a shadowy face poked above the roofline. The man didn't see him at first, for he was looking down, perhaps at someone else below. Then, as

205

he swung up the ladder on to the roof, he saw Rourke, and stopped in astonishment. At the same time Rourke recognized the uniform. It was the scruffy guard he had glimpsed briefly just before his journey began.

The man said something. Rourke remained silent, at a complete loss. He didn't want to give away the fact that he was foreign, didn't want to reveal his gun and certainly didn't want to use it unless he had to.

The guard began shouting at him. Rourke simply shook his head.

Then the man was silent for a moment. Instantly Rourke guessed what he was thinking. Hours before there had been a fire. The train had stopped. There had been that strange noise out in the desert. And here was an unauthorized character on the roof. *Shifta*! Robber!

With a yell, the guard vanished back down the ladder. Again, Rourke could read his intentions. He had probably been climbing on to the roof to cool down, and maybe have a smoke. He had been completely unprepared for the confrontation. Now he had scurried back inside to find a weapon, and help.

Rourke moved fast. He grabbed his rifle, stood up and jumped the three feet on to the next car – a small gap, but not without its dangers in a 25 m.p.h. wind. His first aim was to get as far away as possible from the guard and his mate. With luck, he would be able to slip down between the first freight-car and the engine. If he had to, he would jump off. He didn't relish the prospect. Out in the desert he would for a few seconds be a clear target, even in moonlight, and anyway they might have some way of stopping the train. Best evade them as long as possible.

As it happened, he didn't have to. They spotted him before he reached the end of the leading freight-car. Rourke, who had been casting glances behind him, saw first one, then the other, emerge on to the roof. They were carrying guns. One of them yelled at him. Possibly they hadn't yet seen he was armed. That gave him a few more seconds' grace. He flattened himself on the roof, still keeping his rifle hidden by holding it tight against his body, but slipped the safety-catch off, ready to fire if he had to.

Two coaches away, the two guards seemed uncertain what to do. One stood up, and jumped across to the next coach. His mate followed. They knelt down, as if waiting for Rourke to make a move. He did nothing.

Now number one, presumably the senior, shouted at Rourke again, gesticulating with his gun.

'No way, sunshine,' muttered Rourke, but did nothing.

Something flipped in number one. Perhaps he was too nervous to approach further, suspecting that the odd, silent *shifta* had a weapon of some kind. He raised his own weapon, but warily, probably intending to advance while keeping his intended prisoner covered.

For Rourke, the risks were too high. In those conditions – darkness, wind, shaking coach, no night-sights – there was little chance of being hit, but he didn't fancy staring down the barrel of a gun for no good reason.

Even as number one raised his gun, Rourke slid his weapon into position, aimed as well as he could, though he could not even see his sights clearly, and fired. He had great advantages – training, conviction, a firm position – and they told. The man screamed, toppled sideways, overbalanced in the wind, and rolled off the edge of the roof. He hit the ground with a thump. Rourke had a final glimpse of him rolling away sideways, then vanishing behind a bush.

Number two stood as if transfixed, his windblown head haloed in moonlit hair, and made no move even to raise his weapon. Rourke thought: this guy's about to crack. He fired a shot, deliberately wide. The man dropped his gun, which clattered away over the edge of the roof, and clasped his chest in a caricature gesture of imminent death, then, without a sound, leaped into the darkness. Personally, Rourke would rather have a fire-fight than make a jump like that into the unknown. Still, he made it. Rourke saw him land, somersault and roll to a standstill.

The train rumbled on. Rourke was alone with his thoughts, the darkness, the wind and the shaking carriage roof below him. It was as if nothing had happened. But he didn't like it. There was a carriage full of passengers back there. Some of them must have seen the guards leave, return, grab weapons, climb out again. They must have heard the shots, the screams, the thump of the falling body on the roof. Even if they had all decided just to sit there, somebody would probably do something at the next stop.

Right: no stop.

He turned, decisively – and there, on top of the engine, was the driver. He was standing, unsteadily, and he seemed to have only one arm. For a second, Rourke could not make sense of the sight. Then he understood: the man's other arm was raised in front of him, seemingly a part of his shadowy form. Rourke could tell the arm was raised, because as he now saw from the glint of moon on metal, it held a pistol.

As the driver fired, Rourke threw himself flat. He was icy calm, on home ground. He knew that a man with a pistol standing on shaking foundations had precious little chance of hitting anything, even in daylight. He pulled the carbine up into his shoulder. This took time. As he aimed, the man fired again. To Rourke's surprise, the bullet zinged off the metal just by his left elbow, which was already cradling the

Williams. He fired. It was a large target, and he knew he had hit his mark. This guy was made of different stuff. He crumpled, but supported himself with one hand, aimed shakily with the other, and fired again. Rourke returned fire. Lucky shot. A spray of something soft left the man's head, and he fell backwards, to lie unmoving along the top of his engine.

The train rolled on.

The problem was: no driver.

Well, thought Rourke, that's one way of ensuring we don't make the next stop. What now?

He ran along the top of the engine, to the driver. The man was not in good shape, having lost half his head. Rourke hesitated for only a moment. He would have some explaining to do anyway, and didn't fancy making things worse by arriving wherever he was going with a corpse aboard. He rolled the body sideways until it slumped off the engine.

He stood back, braced himself against the shaking and the gusting wind, and ran forward towards the cab. He noticed how sure-footed he had become. He was above the driver's cab fast and easily. It was not enclosed, like normal diesels, but half open, like a steam train, shaded from the sun, but well ventilated. Presumably the bit that he was on, from which ran an access ladder into the cab, held the fuel. At the front was the engine itself. He had put down the carbine and was about to descend the ladder when he realized why he was able to move so sure-footedly, why he had been able to hit the driver so easily. It was getting light. In the heat of battle, he simply hadn't registered the fact. He stared round. Yes, he could see over twilit grey to the horizon. Behind, no sign of mountains. He turned to look ahead – and he saw low buildings, cars, people. A station.

He scrambled down into the cab, lifting the carbine down beside him. His main aim was not to get at the controls – it would take time to work them out – but to keep out of sight.

He caught only a glimpse as they rumbled through the stop. He heard a sort of communal groan, saw hands raised. There was quite a crowd. He wondered how many the train could take, or whether perhaps they were waiting not as passengers but for the contents of the freight-cars. Whatever, they were history now. Ahead lay more desert, the border, and more trouble.

Because a runaway train tends to draw attention. Forget the fact that three Ethiopians had been scattered along the track, one of whom would be eager to tell his story. Behind him he had two bunches of disappointed people, one lot at the station, another lot riding along with him, in the rear carriage. Some of them, presumably, would have been expecting to get off. Now he had ruined their weekend. Someone would make a fuss. Up ahead, he could expect an interesting reception.

He stared at the array of throttles, levers and knobs on the dashboard. All the gauges were in Squiggly – Arabic, Amharic, something. One pointer hovered erratically around '40'. Kilometres per hour, probably. Other gauges indicated various levels and pressures, but there was no way of knowing what they measured.

One good thing: four flasks hung from hooks above him. Suddenly realizing just how much he needed water, he grabbed one and drank, feeling relief spread through him. He drank until he could drink no more, then forced himself to drink again. There was a whole day to get through, and he would need his eight pints.

It seemed to him that to make the best of a bad job he should probably stop somewhere short of the border. What then? Head off across the desert, find a shady spot, rest up, sneak over at night? Ridiculous. The heat was already building, and the landscape was as forbidding as ever. Not flat now, he noticed – the track led through hills of tortured, jagged outcrops – but equally forbidding.

He tentatively pulled a lever, hoping it might be the accelerator. The engine let out a foghorn bellow. Great. Now the whole fucking desert knew he was on his way.

He looked ahead, through a little side window, and saw it was pointless to make plans, because there, less than half a mile away, was the border. It had to be. Two flag-poles, platforms, two low buildings, a siding, another train waiting. And a barrier pole across the track.

He stared as if mesmerized, knowing there was simply nothing he could do about what was about to happen. The track was clear, no one was going to get hurt. He smiled at the thrill of it. He was living a schoolboy dream, a made-for-TV movie. What a way to leave the country! They had planned everything to be secret, and here he was on the verge of creating an international incident. The long-term impact – how he was going to stop the train, whether Djibouti would put the army on to him, how he would get back to London, whether he would get any of the cash he had been promised, what the Regiment would do about it – none of that mattered. He was living for the moment, and he loved it.

In fact, when the moment came, he hardly noticed. It would have looked good on camera, with the red and white barrier pole splintering, officials waving, street traders with food, drink and trinkets open-mouthed. But Rourke's view was limited. A mere glimpse of flying wood, a blur of buildings and people, and he was through.

Djibouti, he remembered, was a small place, hardly more than the capital and its hinterland of wilderness. It was a port.

So he was already near the coast, maybe twenty, maybe fifty miles to go.

An hour at least, time enough to experiment with the controls, and find out how to stop the thing before he drove over the dockside into the sea. He would try each handle in turn, producing a series of slight responses in the engine, thus building information and experience.

'Hey!' The shout jerked him round. He was already reaching for the carbine, without even identifying where the cry had come from, when it came again. 'Hey! Do you speak English?'

Rourke paused, and looked up. There, peering into the cab, was the face of a man: young, early twenties probably, blue eyes above stubble. But it was the language that stopped Rourke dead – that and the accent. Eton, Oxford, Guards. Not a 'Rupert' – as the SAS squaddies called their officers – but certainly Rupert material.

Rourke controlled his astonishment. 'Yes,' he shouted. There was a lot of noise, what with the wind and the engine and the rattling wheels. He signalled: Get down here.

The figure nodded, and swung down the ladder. Yes, a fit bloke, dressed in wide shorts and a black T-shirt. Well, he would have to be to make the climb from the rear carriage, which was where Rourke assumed he came from.

'Terrific,' said the Rupert with a grin. 'What luck. An Ethiopian train driver who speaks English.'

'I *am* English, you prat,' Rourke replied.

The Rupert stared up and down at the local costume and the bare feet, then back at the face.

'Good heavens. So you are. Well.' Rourke could almost hear the sound of old assumptions being dumped, and new ones slamming into place. 'Gibbs. Christopher Gibbs.'

'Hi.' Rourke paused. He wondered briefly about his mission and his supposed identity. Fuck it. That was over. Right now he needed all the help he could get. He might not tell the whole truth, but he needed to tell some of it. 'Michael Rourke. Now listen. There's a problem.'

'Ah.'

'The engine. Do you know anything about engines?'

'You're the driver,' said Gibbs. 'I just came to find out what's going on.'

Rourke's expression did not change. 'I am *not* the fucking driver,' he snapped. 'The fucking driver is dead. I blew his head off. This train is out of control, and we have to stop it.'

Gibbs had been through a number of surprises in the last minute. He seemed to take it well.

'Ah,' he said again. He registered the carbine. 'Are you in trouble?'

'A bit. I've killed at least one, maybe two, of the locals and I've hijacked a train I can't control. You could call it trouble.'

'Do you make a habit of this sort of thing?' Gibbs was clearly wary of asking outright the question that was bothering him: Are you a violent criminal on the run? Should I be frightened?

Rourke had to come up with something to reassure him, or risk losing his help. 'MI5,' he said. 'I was trying to leave the country discreetly. There was trouble. I lost a couple of friends. I had to improvise.'

'Good heavens. Well, that explains one or two things.'

Rourke liked him. Gibbs was clearly used to coping with the unusual. Rourke glanced out of the front window again, wondering how much longer they had. 'Tell me,' he said, turning back to the controls and reaching for a lever.

'Well, I was back there with Stella and the baby . . .'

'You brought a *baby* into this hole?'

'What's wrong with that? It's a regular service, you know. Besides, it's the cheapest way to Djibouti. We're picking up a boat there.'

Rourke paused, his hand on the lever. He had some adapting of his own to do. He had dropped out of civilization two days ago, and assumed that its benefits were way ahead. It was a shock to realize there were ordinary people following a regular lifestyle right there, with him.

'Anyway,' continued Gibbs, then broke off. 'Shouldn't we be doing something?'

'I'm doing it,' Rourke said. 'You talk.' What Gibbs had to say might give him a clue about how to proceed.

Gibbs was an anthropologist, returning from a dig in the Rift. His words stirred in Rourke vague memories of what he had learned when setting up the fuel dumps. He and his family were experienced travellers, and had actually made this trip a couple of times before. Stella and baby Joe had been rocking in their seats asleep, like everyone else, when they had been disturbed by the sudden action, the back and forth of the guards and the trouble on the roof. All was darkness, of course, because the lights were down, but Gibbs had heard the gunfire, and the two men had not returned. Nothing seemed amiss, however, so he and Stella had dismissed their fears for a while, until the train rattled through the station and then crashed through the frontier. That was serious. Gibbs had asked around. This was an international trip, so among the forty-odd passengers was a scattering of foreigners: Germans, French, English-speaking Arabs, and one American, a UN aid worker. All were worried. Gibbs, the fittest and most experienced, took it upon himself to find out what was happening.

'So,' he finished. 'I'd better get back.'

'Not yet.' Rourke had tried a number of switches and levers. He knew the hooter, of course, and now, although he wasn't sure what he had tried, he knew he had not found the throttle or the brakes. But there weren't many more levers and buttons to try. One of them would probably be an emergency stop. He didn't want that. 'Listen. I don't want to get arrested.'

'I bet.'

'I need your help.'

'Ah. How did I guess?'

'You know the place. Got any ideas?'

'Yes, as a matter of fact.'

Rourke hauled on a lever. There was a grinding noise from the wheels, and the train shuddered. He had found the brakes. But they were still under power. He released the lever again.

'Good show,' said Gibbs. 'Try this one.'

'I'm going to, OK? Just tell me about Djibouti.'

'Quite small. Taxis. A few embassies.'

'So all I need to do is hop off, get a cab, and say "British consulate",' Rourke said drily, trying another lever. The sound of the engine rose. The train began to gain speed. The throttle! He moved the lever the opposite way. The train began to slow. He wondered if there was a clutch as well. Apparently not: probably the engine simply disengaged at low revs.

'Progress,' commented Gibbs. 'Well, there's no British rep here. The Yanks do that job. You should be OK as long as you choose a spot not too far outside town. There's a sort of shanty area that might give you some cover. But you won't get much joy from a cabby dressed like that.'

Rourke grimaced.

'I've got a jacket you can borrow,' said Gibbs decisively. 'And a pair of sandals. Hang on.'

He reached for the ladder.

'One more thing,' said Rourke. 'Got any cash?'

'Enough for a cab.'

'Local currency?'

'Francs. It'll do.' Gibbs glanced out, and started to climb. 'I have to move fast.'

'Better if I stopped. You could run along the track.'

For answer, Gibbs nodded meaningfully to the west, and vanished. Following his gaze, Rourke saw a flashing blue light, then another, heading south fast. There was no doubting their purpose: as he watched, he saw the cars stop, reverse, turn, and drive off northwards. They were tracking the train.

No slowing down yet, then.

Around him, tin-roofed shacks appeared, joined by rough tracks. Steadily, as the train maintained its skaky progress, the density of dwellings increased, until the desert had become mere scars between the shacks.

Rourke waited with growing tension for Gibbs to reappear. The main road, along which the police cars were heading, began to close in on the railway, until he could hear the wail of sirens. Another couple of minutes and they would be right beside him, and any chance of a secretive getaway would be lost.

'Mike!' It was Gibbs, almost falling down beside him. 'Get that thing' – he indicated the *shamma* – 'off, and this on.' He opened out his bundle, which turned out to be a dusty, crumpled colonial-style white jacket wrapped around some sandals. There's a couple of hundred francs in the pocket. So's my card. I expect a drink from you some day.'

'Jesus, can I still do it?' asked Rourke, executing a high-speed change of clothes.

'Yes. The road bends away from the track up ahead, when we start going along the coast. What you have to do is scoot

216

down to the shoreline, and lie low. You don't want the passengers to see you.'

To their right, Rourke saw a wonderful sight. The low, rocky foreshore was yards away, giving on to a ribbon of sand. And there, to the skyline, was the Red Sea. A tanker was heading away from a curve of land out past two dhows. He had been so immersed in drab desert colours and desiccating heat that to see such an immensity of blue water shocked him briefly into immobility.

'Move!' said Gibbs. 'Now!'

Rourke hit the only two levers that mattered. The engine died, the brakes seized, and the wheels locked with shrieks and groans of protest as they slid along the tracks.

'What about you?' Rourke shouted, gripping the side of the cab.

'I'll be OK. The driver was killed, the killer vanished, I found the cab empty, and stopped the train. I'll be a hero!' Gibbs grinned. 'But take this . . .' As the train squealed to a halt, he tossed the *shamma* over Rourke's shoulder. 'And that.' He pointed to the carbine. 'I don't want any evidence!'

'Thanks. Next time we meet, I'll buy.'

'You certainly will. Now go!'

Rourke grabbed the gun, leaped down, and ran as quickly as his sandals would allow to the foreshore. In five seconds, he was down, invisible to the train, among rocks.

He heard sirens, the roar of car engines, the shriek of brakes, loud voices.

He glanced round. Gibbs had been right. There was nothing on this side of the track. No one had seen him. But he couldn't risk staying there. Besides, it was the beginning of another searing day, and among those rocks he would be grilled meat in hours.

But when he moved, he could not afford to attract attention. He buried the rifle, the one remaining magazine and the *shamma* in the sand, and hauled a few rocks over the spot. One day, perhaps, after a storm, some astonished local would find them, and praise Allah for his good fortune.

He felt in the pocket of his newly acquired jacket, which was not a bad fit. No shirt, of course, but good enough for a cab ride. There was the money, two 100-franc notes, and Gibbs's card: an address in London, care of a university department, and a box number in Addis Ababa.

He lay there, feeling the sun beating down, and looked at the card. His training told him to memorize the information, and destroy the card, because to be caught with it would incriminate a colleague. On the other hand, he had no identity at all. It might, perhaps, come in useful.

He began to work his way northwards, along the foreshore, away from the train. He took care to keep low. He could hear nothing now. Gibbs was playing out his role as hero.

And who would gainsay him? Many people could vouch for the ambush out in the desert, which was obviously when the bandit had boarded; all would vouch for the rooftop fight, the fate of the two guards; a brief search would reveal the dead driver; and it was only logical that a fleeing criminal would jump off some time before the border, leaving the train to rumble on unattended, until Gibbs daringly made his climb along the roof to the cab. Perhaps he could even explain his brief return as a mission to reassure his wife and the other passengers. It could make some sort of sense, for a while at least. And certainly it would take even longer to tie up a train hijack in the desert with the disappearance of the Emperor.

A quarter of a mile from the train, he risked a peep over the rocks. Before him lay the railway track. Despite his low-profile view, he could see between the houses – larger ones now, some villas, some apartment blocks – that the road, busy with cars and pedestrians, approached it closely, then crossed it. At this point, buildings blocked his view, sweeping round to crown the peninsula from behind which he had seen the tanker emerging earlier.

He decided to risk exposure. He rose, dusted sand from his trousers and jacket, and walked towards the buildings. He followed a wire fence, and found himself on a paved road. A road sign in Arabic and French told him he was in Ave. M. Lyautey. There was a junction to his left, and just beyond it the level crossing he had seen from the beach. The railway must lead to the station, he thought, and at the station there will be cabs. He was among a mixture of apartment blocks and offices. Few people were on the streets, but about half were in loose European dress. He was a mess, but not a spectacle. No one gave him a second glance.

The station was an early-twentieth-century monument to French colonialism: built of imported stone, ornate, imposing. It was also in an uproar. Street traders blocked the entrance, men and women in Arab dress milled about among them. They had, after all, been waiting for a train that had not yet arrived, and no doubt word had already spread of violence aboard.

But the consequence was that the ramshackle cabs baking in the heat had had no custom. Rourke went to the first in line, and said the magic words: 'American Embassy.' The driver, in flowing Arab gear, nodded in relief, for his long wait was over.

'You take francs?'

'*Des francs? Naturellement, monsieur.*'

The taxi, a 1960s Citroën, swung round and turned out on to the road by which Rourke had arrived. He had imagined

219

himself in the centre. Apparently, not so. The cab headed south, along the road which Rourke had already seen from a distance. There was only one road. Within half a mile, there again was the level crossing, and there – easily visible, not fifty yards from the road, which was almost blocked by cars and trucks – was the train, surrounded now by most of Djibouti's police force. Rourke could even see a TV crew.

'What's happening?' he asked.

The cab driver, his English tested to the limits, shrugged: 'They say, a crazy with gun. Bourn, bourn, train stop.'

Rourke sank back into his seat. He hoped Gibbs would get credit. You didn't get many Ruperts like that outside the Service.

As the cab negotiated a central area neatly laid out in turn-of-the-century stonework, Rourke focused on his story. He had no identity papers or cards, so he needed an exit document and a ticket home. It would not be easy. He had to ensure he was not connected with the business on the train. But in that case how did he get into the country? Lies would rapidly land him in trouble. There was no way he could say anything convincing about a spurious business, a flight, a hotel. And the truth, even if it was believed, would lead back to the train. That opened dire prospects: the Djibouti police, charges, extradition back to Addis.

The US Embassy proved to be a substantial new place, set in a compound, and well protected by a high wall. The State Department had taken advantage of its closeness with France to create a listening post in this strategic spot. The whole area was a political powder keg, with Suez to the north, Saudi Arabia and the volatile Yemen just opposite, and all the surrounding countries – Egypt, Somalia, Ethiopia, Sudan – up for grabs in the Cold War. Hence the heavy-duty iron gates, the guardroom inside, and the barbed-wired walls.

He paid the cab, and was worried to find his 200 francs cut almost in half by the transaction.

He rang a bell. A lugubrious Arab in a business suit emerged from the guard post. 'British,' Rourke explained. 'My passport was stolen.' He handed over Gibbs's card. The man vanished into his guardroom, made a phone call, and pressed a button. One of the gates swung slowly open. Rourke was in.

By the time he had crossed the courtyard, entered the embassy, stood for a few seconds to drink in the bliss of its air-conditioning, and knocked, as instructed, on the first door on the left in the hall, he had his approach ready. He had to go to the top.

The receptionist, a local girl, called her boss, the Personnel Officer. She summoned the Duty Officer, who brought in Immigration. At each stage, Rourke explained that he was an academic compromised by Soviet intelligence in Ethiopia, and that he had driven into Djibouti in a hired car. The car, together with his wallet, passport and all his possessions had just been stolen. He needed US help to repatriate him. Of course, the key to the story was the exact nature of the 'compromise by Soviet intelligence' and he refused to be drawn on this by anyone but the Ambassador himself. He suggested, with some conviction, that what he had to say was so astonishing and significant that it had to be for the ears of the top man. It took two hours to convince them. By then, Rourke, having consumed five glasses of water, was much restored.

The Ambassador was a career diplomat, in his late fifties. He was a time-server, in place to oil the wheels of diplomacy. The real power was held by the intelligence officer, a CIA man in his mid-thirties whose ostensible job was vetting passport applications.

Rourke was eventually confronted by the two of them together. To them, Rourke told the truth. It was easier that way, and he could ensure a degree of control by presenting his information in the order of his choice and by making requests at strategic moments.

First, he told of his arrival in Addis. US diplomats and intelligence sources in Addis would be able to confirm a few essential details: the flight from London, the stay at the Hilton under the assumed names, the use of the Swiss Embassy.

He told them his real name, and his real occupation, and said he was concerned to tell his parents that he was all right. He gave phone numbers. The steely young CIA man, whose name was Barrow, went to make the calls, for it was an easy way to check immediately on the truth of his statement. There was no point in any other calls. The Regiment would disown him, and Cromer would deny all knowledge.

'And now,' he said when Barrow returned. 'You might like to know the purpose of this trip.'

He enjoyed that: talking about the Emperor being still alive, Cromer's plan to kidnap him, his own expedition to dump fuel along the helicopter route south. The two men opposite were riveted.

Just before he started on the story of his escape and the Emperor's death, he got what he needed: a promise of diplomatic immunity and a booking on the afternoon Air France flight to Paris, and on to London.

So then he told them the rest, all of it.

At the end, Barrow asked: 'How much did you tell Gibbs?'

'Nothing. We didn't have much time for chat.'

'So who knows the truth of all this?'

'The top Ethiopians. Cromer. That's it.'

'Fascinating. So much, yet so little.'

'What?'

'It will all, of course, remain secret.'

'Fair enough.'

'Hear me out. Clearly, your role must never be known. Mengistu is not a nice man. He would blame you for killing his golden goose. You would be a marked man for the rest of your life. And perhaps Sir Charles Cromer might not be too happy to have you around, either. Best lie low, Mr Rourke.'

Rourke made no response for a long moment. It was the first time he had really considered his own future. 'Right,' he said.

Barrow hadn't finished. The US also had an interest. If the West was to retain any influence in Ethiopia, it would not do to reveal the Ethiopian plot to keep Selassie alive after they had said he was dead. What, after all, had changed? The Emperor had been declared dead in August 1975, and his money was securely in the West. Now he really was dead, and his money was still there. In the end, Western interests would be best served by pretending nothing had happened.

'So you see, Mr Rourke, we hold each other hostage. If we talk, it's political suicide. If you talk, it's suicide for real. Do we have a deal?'

There was just one problem before he left: who would pay?

Rourke could hardly believe what he was hearing. He was giving them the inside story of the century, and they worried about the cost of a flight to London.

'I know. Petty, huh? We can drive you to the airport, but flights are something else. We have accounts committees, and you can see why we don't exactly want to be up front about you. So help us. You have cash? Cards?'

'No.'

223

'Anyone you want to call?'

There was only one person who might, with luck, guarantee him the cost of a plane fare.

They allowed him to call. He called the shop, for its number was imprinted on his mind.

'Lucy?'

'Mike.' She sighed, as if he'd been a naughty boy. 'I thought I told you not to call the shop.'

'It's an emergency. Listen . . .' And he told her where he was and what was required.

'Tell me, Mike,' she said. 'Why am I doing this?'

'For the same reason I'm asking. I don't want to go away again. I want you to meet me at the airport.'

There was a pause.

'I'll be there,' she said.

Epilogue

Rourke's escapade had significant consequences, some short-term and secret, some long-term and anything but secret.

News of his escape with the Emperor reached Mengistu in minutes. Within hours, the Bell's flight path had been identified, and the helicopter had been found. At first it seemed that both the Emperor and Rourke must have perished. The chances were that a weak old man and an inexperienced foreigner – there was no way of knowing that Rourke was in fact a member of the SAS – would not survive for long in the desert, without food and water. Within a few days, when the report came through of the Emperor's body being found in the desert, Mengistu revised his conclusions marginally. The odd business of a lone *shifta* hijacking a train caused him to wonder, but there was no evidence to link those events with Rourke. He had apparently vanished, to become food for the vultures.

Cromer's role in all this was realized immediately. In one way, Cromer was relieved. Things had worked out well for him, if in ways he could never have predicted. There was no need after all to renegotiate a complex contract with Selassie, no need to make secretive, expensive and politically explosive arrangements for Selassie's well-being. At a stroke, the fortune was safe. He did not even have to pay out any more to Collins, Halloran and Rourke.

Cromer naturally offered specious apologies to Mengistu for the extraordinary behaviour of his banking colleagues. Of course he denied all knowledge of their agenda. As a face-saving gesture and sign of his continuing goodwill, he at once offered a $200 million loan, which was accepted.

The public consequences of the plot were brought about by Mengistu, who was not only ruthless, but fast-thinking and astute, a true survivor. He had from the start promised a revolution, national security, and the funds to fuel both.

At first, he had put his faith in the Americans, for Moscow was committed to Ethiopia's hostile neighbour, Somalia. Despite his adherence to Marxism, he had made no immediate break with the USA. American advisers had remained. In early 1976 came the possibility of wealth from Selassie. Mengistu made more promises: with Western coop-eration he would end famine, secure the borders, defeat the enemy.

Cromer's duplicity and Rourke's astonishing actions tipped the balance. In anger, and in defence of his own political position, he prepared a new pro-Soviet policy.

The change came in late 1976. Mengistu used much of Cromer's loan as a down payment on Russian arms. Moscow was amazed, and delighted to receive such an approach from a country that could dominate North-East Africa as Somalia never would. Somalia was repudiated, Ethiopia vaunted as Moscow's true friend. In early 1977, the Americans were thrown out. For the next decade, Ethiopia became the strongest Soviet satellite in Africa.

There has always been a debate about just how much difference an individual can make on events. Normally, the debate focuses on the rich and powerful. Here, however, was a case in which one ordinary man, seeking nothing but his own safety, changed the course of recent history.